"No one is more concerned for the safety of the train and its passengers than I am," Nicholas spoke quietly into the strange, strained silence.

"But what I cannot seem to make you understand is that I couldn't move the trains into the tunnel even if I thought that was best . . ."

As the enormity of what he was saying sank in, Ginny could hear one of the women begin to weep quietly. They were trapped. Stuck fast, with the great snowfield rising straight up above them.

Ginny stared across the room at Nicholas's tired, desperate face. Without warning, she shivered. Goosebumps tingled along the surface of her skin. In her heart, even in the midst of her love, a terrible fear began to blossom.

There was a reason she couldn't see the future, and it had nothing to do with the situation with Virginia. Ginny couldn't see the future because there wasn't going to be one. She was going to lose everything in this cold, forbidding place.

She was going to die at Wellington.

Look for these historical romance titles
from Archway Paperbacks

Hindenburg, 1937 by Cameron Dokey
San Francisco Earthquake, 1906 by Kathleen Duey
The Great Chicago Fire, 1871 by Elizabeth Massie
Washington Avalanche, 1910 by Cameron Dokey

Washington
AVALANCHE
1910

CAMERON DOKEY

AN ARCHWAY PAPERBACK
Published by POCKET BOOKS
New York London Toronto Sydney Singapore

AN ARCHWAY PAPERBACK *Original*

An Archway Paperback published by
POCKET BOOKS, a division of Simon & Schuster Inc.
1230 Avenue of the Americas, New York, NY 10020

Copyright © 2000 by Mary Cameron Dokey

ISBN: 0-671-03604-1

First Archway Paperback printing March 2000

10 9 8 7 6 5 4 3 2 1

AN ARCHWAY PAPERBACK and colophon are registered trademarks of Simon & Schuster Inc.

Cover art by Sandy Young/Studio Y

Printed in the U.S.A.

IL 7+

For the people who first taught me to love trains, my maternal grandparents Hazel M. and George W. Johnson. And for the person who still teaches me how to watch for spring, my paternal grandmother, Mabel A. Dokey.

❧ PROLOGUE ❧

Eastern Washington State
February 21, 1910

Snow was falling.

Not fat, lacy flakes for catching on the tongue or rolling into snowmen, but fine, hard-scoured pellets of frozen water dropping out of a sheet-white sky.

The wind caught it, dashing it against the windows of houses in the towns with a sound like fingers desperately scratching. Whirled it high up into the air before flinging it down at last, allowing it to settle into high drifts in the already piled high frozen yards.

Old folks shook their heads and said it couldn't be good, a storm so strong this late in the season. Not after a winter that had already been as bad as even the oldest of them could recall.

In the Cascade mountains separating east from west, the snowdrifts lay as high as twenty feet in the passes where the tracks of the Great Northern Railway came through, twisting and turning like a snake to connect one part of Washington state with the other.

Railroad men in stops along the route stared out at the weather, then told themselves there was no need to worry. They'd faced tough storms before. There'd never been one yet that had kept the trains from running. Surely this storm was just the last hurrah of a bitter winter. Storms this late in the season were always short. This one would prove no different. It would soon expend its fury.

They blew their lanterns out, climbed into their hard beds, pulled the covers up to their chins, closed their eyes, and told themselves it would probably all be over by the morning.

But all that night, like a thick, white shroud dropping from the darkened heavens, the snow kept falling.

ॐ 1 ॐ

"Virginia Nolan! What in heaven's name do you think you're doing?"

At the sound of her stepsister-in-law's voice, Ginny Nolan jumped, cracking her head against the window frame. A clump of hard-packed snow dislodged above her, landing squarely on the back of her neck.

Ginny could feel its wet coldness sliding downward, penetrating the thin, high collar of her shirt waist. Quickly, she jerked back. Her action tumbled more fresh snow onto the perfectly polished hardwood floor of Amanda Banks's front parlor.

Now I've done it, Ginny thought. Next to her four-year-old son, Mason, her stepsister-in-law's house was her most prized possession. That and the sterling reputation of the family name. The Banks were an important family in Spokane, and Amanda never let anyone forget it, particularly Ginny, since she wasn't one of them.

"Oh, for mercy's sake, Ginny," Amanda Banks exclaimed now, her tone sharp with irritation. "Snow on the floor will ruin the finish, and Emily just did this room this morning."

With an angry twitch of skirts, head held high as a queen's, Amanda strode forward into the front parlor, heading toward the bell pull she could use to summon a servant. Even through her annoyance with herself, Ginny had to admit her stepsister-in-law looked impressive.

Unlike Ginny, Amanda was always conscious of the impression she made. It was an important part of keeping up appearances. And Ginny was sure keeping up appearances was the only thing that kept her stepsister-in-law from making her clean up the soggy mess she'd made herself.

It would never do to have a member of the family perform such a menial task, even an unimportant family member, such as Ginny.

"Though why you would want to open a window in the middle of a snowstorm—" Amanda went on as she gave the cord so hard an angry yank that Ginny could swear she heard the bell at the other end, ringing in the kitchen "—I'm sure I cannot possibly imagine. It's never been so cold, not for twenty years. Stephen said so at breakfast just this morning. But, naturally, it's too much to hope that you were paying attention. You never listen to a word we say."

That's not true, Ginny thought. *I listened plenty last night.* Even more than the ice still melting down her back, the thought of what she'd heard made her shiver.

Quickly, she turned away from Amanda's petulant face, pulling the window closed with one swift, hard movement. Her action caused a final clump of snow to tumble to the floor at her feet. From behind her, Ginny heard Amanda make a strangled sound of dismay.

"It's been all I could do to keep the house a decent temperature since this storm set in yesterday," she went on, her voice shrill, "even with a fire going in almost every room. Mason could catch a chill indoors, and you know how I worry about his health.

"I might have hoped, having lost your own so young yourself, that you'd have some respect for a mother's feelings. But it appears that I hoped for too much, as usual. You have no respect for the feelings of others. After all your brother and I have done for you, too. You don't know the half of it, let me tell you that."

Stepbrother, Ginny thought, her eyes still fixed on the storm swirling outside the window. *Stephen is no true relation of mine, Amanda, and neither are you.*

But her stepsister-in-law had been right about one thing, Ginny thought now, as she reluctantly turned back to face her. Ginny didn't know the *half* of what her stepbrother and his wife had done for her. She knew it all. She knew everything. All the things Stephen and Amanda Banks had planned for Virginia Nolan's future. A future they'd designed to cover up their own past misdeeds.

Just thinking about it still had the power to make Ginny's throat close up in some strange combination of fury and terror. Realizing how close she'd come to never knowing the truth made her blood run colder than even the snowstorm's rage. If it hadn't been for the fact that she'd been unable to sleep late last night and had come downstairs in search of a book—

Don't think about that now, she told herself, appalled to discover that her hands were shaking. Quickly, she thrust them behind her back where Amanda couldn't see them.

The action made her feel like a penitent schoolgirl standing meekly before an angry headmistress, an image she was sure her stepsister-in-law would appreciate. Amanda was always happy to provide instruction to others, her two favorite recipients being her servants and Ginny.

Don't think about anything but placating Amanda, Ginny told herself sternly. The sooner she mended things with her stepsister-in-law, the safer she would be. Then Amanda would go back to ignoring her the way she usually did. Being the center of Amanda's attention was the last thing Ginny wanted, particularly today.

"I'm sorry, Amanda," she said now, stepping away from the window, being careful to avoid the snow rapidly melting into a slushy puddle. Perhaps putting some distance between herself and the scene of her transgression would make her apology more effective.

"You're absolutely right. Opening a window was foolish and thoughtless of me. It's just—"

Just what? she asked herself, sardonically. How did she think she could explain her feelings to Amanda, even if she'd been in the habit of confiding in her? Even if confiding in her had been safe?

How on earth could she tell her stepsister-in-law how intolerable she found it to stay inside her house now that she knew what Amanda and Stephen had done? What they still intended to do. How could she tell Amanda that she could hardly bear to look at her? That all she wanted was to get away?

Ginny had lain awake for hours last night, trying to formulate a plan of action, desperately turning over various plans of escape. She'd wanted to run straight out of the house after she'd overheard Stephen and Amanda's conversation. But, even in her outrage and fear, she'd known she couldn't act so precipitously. She couldn't afford to give herself away.

It was the only reason Ginny was still in the house today. The only reason she'd endured the agonizing hours from breakfast until luncheon, from luncheon until mid-afternoon. She knew she had to choose her time for action carefully. She would have only one chance to get away.

In the hour after Stephen came home in the late afternoon, while he and Amanda were in their own rooms dressing for dinner. Not until then could Ginny act upon her plan to escape. To go earlier was to risk detection. That was what Ginny had told herself in the dark, bleak hours of the early morning.

But she hadn't reckoned on how difficult things would be today.

To spend the day as always, doing nothing, pretending to know nothing. Inactivity had made Ginny's body sore, like a toothache. She'd been so desperate she'd finally resorted to working on her embroidery, a ladylike activity of which Amanda wholeheartedly approved, but which Ginny usually hated.

It hadn't helped a bit.

Instead of soothing her nerves, the close, tiny stitches Ginny was creating only served to remind her of how close and narrow her world would become if she didn't get away. But it wasn't until she'd thrust her needle into her finger hard enough to draw blood that she'd abandoned the embroidery and taken the drastic step of opening the window.

She'd hoped the bitter weather would distract her from her bitter thoughts. She'd never intended to leave the window open for more than a few seconds. Even she knew it was too cold a day. It was just plain bad luck that Amanda had come back downstairs, after seeing young Mason put down for his nap, to find Ginny with her head in the snowstorm.

Apologize again, Ginny told herself now. Maybe if she said she was sorry enough times, Amanda would spare her a lecture and let her go up to her room. Ginny didn't think she had the patience to bear one of Amanda's full-fledged harangues today. Her own nerves were too raw. She would be too likely to snap back, and that would ruin everything.

"I *am* sorry, Amanda," she said. "I was just so astonished to see so much snow." Ginny closed her lips abruptly over the words that rose up, threatening to spill over. *And so afraid the storm would stop me*.

Amanda Banks's blue eyes narrowed. Even from across the room, Ginny could tell the expression in them was calculating, and something else. *Good*, she thought. She'd surprised her.

Though she was careful never to be impolite to

CAMERON DOKEY

her stepsister-in-law, Ginny rarely apologized for the misdeeds Amanda laid so constantly at her door. Most of them were simply imaginary. Almost the first lesson Ginny had learned upon coming to live with her stepbrother and his wife was that no matter how she behaved they were always going to find fault with her.

The second thing she'd learned was that Stephen Banks hadn't approved of his mother Edith's marriage to Ginny's father, Abner Nolan. There was only one reason he hadn't opposed it: upon his marriage, Abner had promised to settle all of Edith's debts. The Banks family needed Abner Nolan's money.

Banks was an old, distinguished family name in eastern Washington. Much more distinguished than Nolan. But being distinguished was no longer the same as being wealthy. Abner Nolan could provide the money the Banks so desperately needed if they were going to keep up the appearances they considered so all-important.

When Abner and Edith had died in a freak accident on their honeymoon, their sailboat overtaken by a sudden summer squall, Stephen had had no choice but to take in Abner's daughter. Ginny's own mother had died when she was a young girl. She had no other relatives.

Not offering her a home would have made the

family look bad, have been a black mark on its spotless reputation. But although Stephen and Amanda had taken Ginny in, they had never made her welcome. Instead, they'd made her feel like what they obviously thought she was: a charity case, an obligation.

From the moment she'd first set foot into her stepbrother's house nearly two years ago, only one thing had kept Ginny going. The knowledge that she didn't have to stay there forever. When she turned eighteen, she would come into the inheritance her mother had left. Then, she'd have enough money to be independent.

Ginny knew it was unusual for young women to live on their own, but as soon as she came into her money, she intended to try it. She didn't want to stay in her stepbrother's house one hour more than she had to.

And now her eighteenth birthday was less than three months away.

Without warning, Ginny shivered, as if just thinking about her approaching birthday had suddenly brought the trap into which her stepbrother hoped to lure her even closer.

I'm not going to step into it, she thought. *Not now that I know the truth.*

"Oh, there you are, Emily," Amanda said as a girl several years younger than Ginny, dressed in the dark skirt, white blouse, and white apron of a household servant, finally appeared in the parlor doorway.

She was panting ever so slightly, as if out of breath. Her pale cheeks were flushed. Tiny tendrils of blond hair had escaped from her cap to curl damply around her face. Looking at her, Ginny felt a pang of guilt. Amanda Banks worked her servants hard, and Ginny hadn't intended to make things harder for any one of them, particularly Emily, who was the youngest.

"Where have you been?" Amanda demanded. If she noticed the girl's rapid breaths, she gave no sign. "You certainly took your time about coming. Tidy yourself up, girl. You look a mess. I've told you I won't have that."

"I'm sorry, ma'am," Emily gasped out, her fingers fumbling to put her hair back into place. "It's just that I was—"

"I've no time to listen to your excuses," Amanda broke in sharply. "Miss Virginia has opened a window and let the snow in all over the floor. I expect you to do something about it."

How cold her voice is, Ginny thought. It was the same tone Amanda had used the night before. Not because she'd been speaking to her husband, but because she'd been speaking about Ginny. *I'm like a servant in her eyes,* Ginny thought. *Beneath her. Expendable.*

In the doorway, Emily bobbed a quick curtsy. "Don't worry, ma'am," she said. "I'll attend to it right away."

"See that you do," Amanda said, as the servant spun on her heel and began to move away. "There's no time to waste. I shouldn't have to tell you that."

A sudden wave of nausea hit Ginny, full in the stomach. She took a few stumbling steps, and sat down hard in the nearest chair, heedless of the fact that she'd sat on top of her own embroidery. The striped wallpaper of the parlor wavered before her eyes.

Amanda had said almost exactly the same thing last night, her cold voice finally warming with urgency.

"Tell Jack he must move faster," she'd told her husband. "That girl's birthday is less than three months away. Everything about this must look proper. It can't look patched up in any way. I shouldn't have to tell you that, Stephen. Jack is dallying, and there's no time to waste."

Ginny closed her eyes, swallowing hard as bile inched with acid fingers up the back of her throat. This was the thing she'd learned last night. The thing that made her whole world different today. Standing in the hallway outside the library, listening to her stepbrother and his wife discuss her until her heart had turned numb and her body icy.

Stephen had been stealing from her, from practically the moment she'd set foot in the house. Robbing her of her inheritance. Her only chance for freedom. He'd planned to pay it back, or so he'd claimed. But his investments had gone sour, and now it was too late. Now, there was only one way out.

Ginny had to marry before her eighteenth birthday.

If she did that, everything she owned would become the property of her husband. Stephen's theft would never come to light. He would be safe.

As long as Ginny had the right husband.

She felt the bile inch a little higher.

She could still hardly believe that laughing, charming Jack Lawton was a part of Stephen's schemes. She still didn't know precisely why. It was likely she'd never know. But Ginny figured she had all the knowledge that she needed.

The knowledge that she'd come too close to believing that she could love Jack, as he claimed to love her. Too close to doing exactly what her stepbrother wished her to do: be swept off her feet.

Because even Ginny had to admit that, in Jack Lawton, Stephen Banks had found the perfect bait. Jack was impetuous and headstrong, just as Ginny was, attributes which had probably led him to become embroiled in Stephen's schemes in the first place.

All Stephen had had to do was to dangle Jack in front of her, and wait for Ginny's own nature to carry her away. It had almost worked. Ginny felt a chill sweep over her. Cold sweat broke out on her forehead.

I won't think about that now, she thought. *I can't. I've got to concentrate on getting through today.*

"Gracious, Ginny," she heard her stepsister-in-law exclaim suddenly. "Are you all right? You've gone as white as a sheet."

Quickly, Ginny opened her eyes. She'd done it again, she thought, attracted attention she didn't want. "I'm fine, thank you, Amanda."

Do something, she thought. *Don't give yourself away.*

"Perhaps I'm the one who's catching a chill," she went on with an attempt at a rueful smile. "No doubt it would serve me right for opening the window."

Instantly, Amanda's expression softened with concern. Once Ginny might have hoped it meant her stepsister-in-law was coming finally to feel more warmly toward her. But not today. Today Ginny knew the truth. Amanda's concern was all for her own schemes. She didn't care at all about Ginny.

But if Ginny fell ill enough to keep to her bed, she might not be able to see Jack Lawton for days.

Such a delay could prove disastrous to what Stephen and Amanda were planning. The timeline was already growing short. Amanda had said so last night.

"Tell Jack he must move faster. Her birthday is less than three months away."

"There now," Amanda said. "We can't have you catching a cold, young lady." She crossed the room with rapid, clicking steps to lay a hand on Ginny's forehead.

"You are a trifle warm," she admitted. "Perhaps you should go upstairs and rest. Jack is coming to dinner this evening, remember," she added, her tone growing playful. "You wouldn't want to miss him, would you? And I know you'll want to look your best."

She urged Ginny to her feet, handing her her embroidery with a gay tinkle of laughter.

"Silly girl," she said. "Now look what you've done. You've sat on your embroidery. I'd say you're growing absent-minded, Ginny, and you know what that means."

That I have more important things to think about? Ginny wondered sarcastically. But she didn't even think of answering in such a way.

"I think I will go up and lie down," she said instead. "Thank you for your concern, Amanda. And I truly am sorry about the floor."

"Oh, well," her stepsister-in-law said with a wave of her hand, her earlier anger seemingly forgotten. She tucked her arm through Ginny's as she guided her out of the parlor and across the downstairs hall. "I daresay this horrible weather has set us all on edge. And accidents do happen."

She's afraid to stay angry with me for too long, Ginny realized suddenly. Amanda and Stephen were always complaining that Ginny was too unpredictable, too impetuous. She might refuse to do what they wanted, if they pushed her too far.

"You have a good long rest," Amanda said, giving Ginny a gentle nudge toward the stairs. "Just nip this little cold right in the bud, Ginny. No man ever proposed to a girl with a red nose, you know."

Again, she gave a peal of bright, false laughter. Ginny forced herself to return the smile. *Jack Lawton is never going to propose to me, Amanda,* she thought as she turned to climb the stairs. *I'm never going to give him the chance.*

Her only regret would be that she'd never get to see the looks on the faces of the three conspirators when they found that she'd vanished.

Ginny reached the top of the stairs. She moved along the upstairs hallway, suddenly grateful for things she'd hardly thought to pay attention to before today.

Like the way the runner of carpet down the very

center of the hallway muffled her footsteps. And the fact that her bedroom was near the head of the stairs.

Until now, Ginny had always taken the placement of her room as an insult, a signal of her less-than-important status in the Banks household. A room near the head of the stairs was much noisier than those farther down the hall.

But today the location of her room would be to her advantage. It meant she wouldn't have to tiptoe past Stephen and Amanda's door when she left the house. Their room was at the very end of the hall. The only potential danger lay in the fact that one of their windows overlooked the street.

Ginny opened her bedroom door and quickly scanned the room. Everything looked the same as always. Only she knew that her carpet bag was packed and waiting in her wardrobe, concealed by her long skirts. By the time Jack arrived for dinner, Ginny would be long gone.

She stepped into the room, closed the door behind her, then went to kneel upon her bed, staring out at the storm.

There were huge loopholes in the scheme Ginny had concocted in the middle of last night. She knew that. She'd also known she didn't have a choice. She couldn't spend another night beneath her stepbrother's roof. He was right. She was impetuous, and sooner or later her impetuous nature would drive her to reveal the fact that she knew what he had done.

But simply leaving Stephen's household wasn't enough. She had to put herself completely beyond his control. That was why, at six o'clock that night, Ginny was taking the boldest step that she could think of: she was going to the train depot. There, she'd board the westbound train that would take her across the mountains to Seattle.

Whether or not she'd ultimately make her home in western Washington's busiest port city, how she'd survive once she got there, Ginny didn't yet know. All she knew was that she was going.

A flurry of snow scraped against the window. Ginny shivered, wrapping her arms around her shoulders. Even through the windowpane, she could feel the cold. She couldn't imagine a worse night than this on which to make a journey.

But she didn't have a choice. She had to go. Nothing could be allowed to stop Virginia Nolan from making her escape. Not her stepbrother. Not his wife. Not the false suitor they'd chosen for her.

Not even the worst storm anyone could remember.

2

"Ginny?"

In the middle of her bedroom, Ginny stopped short, one foot poised in mid-air, the hairs on the back of her neck rising. Surely that was Stephen's voice! He never came to her room, not for any reason. He wouldn't have considered it proper.

But in spite of that fact, he'd come today.

Frantically, Ginny looked around her. If Stephen caught her looking like this, her attempt at escape would be over before it even started. She'd been all but ready to go. Just seconds before the knock on her door, she'd slipped her heaviest winter coat on.

The coat had been the only thing that had gotten her through the rest of the afternoon. Ginny had spent her time sewing what little inheritance she had left, the jewelry that had once belonged to her mother, into the coat's lining.

The only piece she'd saved out was a cameo ring, her father's wedding present to her mother. This she'd slipped onto the ring finger of her right hand, hoping that the token of her parents' love for one another might bring her luck.

But the whole time, Ginny'd kept one ear cocked, listening for the slam of the front door. It was the way Stephen always announced his return to the house.

Amanda hated that Stephen slammed the front door when he came in. She considered such an action vulgar and common. But for once, Stephen disagreed with his wife's notions of proper behavior. As far as he was concerned, everyone should know when the master of the house came home, and nothing accomplished that faster, Stephen said, than a good hard slam of the front door.

Today's slam had come even earlier than usual, a fact which had at first caused Ginny considerable alarm. Had she given herself away somehow? Had Amanda sent word to Stephen saying that Ginny was acting strangely, begging Stephen to return home at once?

She'd bundled the coat into the wardrobe and waited tensely, knowing that she could be summoned at any moment. But nothing had happened. No such summons had come.

Even so, Ginny hadn't relaxed until she'd heard

her stepbrother and his wife actually come upstairs and move past her room along the hall, talking in low voices. They were on their way to their own room, to dress for dinner. At long last, the moment Ginny had spent all afternoon waiting for had come.

She'd given Stephen and Amanda fifteen minutes, the most nerve-wracking fifteen minutes of her life. She'd checked the watch pinned to the front of her shirt waist so often, time hadn't seemed to move at all.

But, finally, the margin of safety Ginny had allowed herself to be certain her stepbrother and his wife really were in their room was over. She'd slipped her coat on and headed for her bedroom door. Her intention had been to open it silently and peek out, to verify that the coast was indeed clear. After that, she'd pin on her hat, retrieve her packed carpet bag and be on her way.

But no sooner had she started across the room than she'd heard the knock on the door.

"Ginny," her stepbrother's voice said once again. "May I come in? It's Stephen."

I know it's you, Stephen, Ginny thought. She felt a desperate giggle of laughter rise up inside her chest, even through her fear. If Stephen wished to come into her room, something very serious must be happening.

Ginny's heart was pounding so hard she could see the front of her coat quiver, but it was the only part of her that seemed able to move. The rest of her was frozen in place in the center of her room.

Do something, her mind commanded. *Take off your coat. Don't let him catch you.*

If Stephen discovered her standing in the middle of her room wearing her heaviest coat, Ginny had absolutely no doubt about what he'd do. He'd see her married to Jack Lawton as soon as possible, even if people talked.

"Ginny! What's the matter? Why don't you answer me?"

In horror, Ginny saw the doorknob move. She made a frantic lunge straight toward the door. She snatched her hat from the top of her dressing table, then spun around and dashed for her bed, frantically stripping off her coat as she did so.

She dove beneath the covers, pulling the coat up to her waist, smashing it down against her hat. Then she pulled her quilt all the way up to her chin, thankful that it was long enough she didn't have to worry about her shoes poking out the bottom.

"Is somebody there?" she called out, doing her best to sound as if he'd just startled her out of a sound sleep. "Did somebody call?"

The door shot inward, as if pushed open with impatient hands. A moment later, her stepbrother appeared in the doorway.

Stephen Banks was a big, imposing man, but Ginny thought her stepbrother had never looked as imposing as he did at this moment. He completely filled her bedroom doorway. His thick, dark eyebrows were pulled together in a frown. His normally pale face was flushed with annoyance.

Ginny began to shiver so hard she had to clench her teeth together to keep them from chattering.

Don't let him see how intimidated you are, she told herself firmly. *Don't let him see that anything is out of the ordinary. You caught a chill. You went upstairs to rest. You did just what Amanda told you to do and no more.*

But still, it took all the courage she possessed for her to face her stepbrother.

Ginny had always thought it was a terrible irony that she and Stephen Banks looked alike, so much so that people meeting them for the first time often mistook them for blood relations. They had the same glossy dark hair, same deep brown eyes. At the moment, Stephen's were snapping with irritation.

"What took you so long to answer?" he demanded, as he came into the room. "Why are you still in bed? You aren't that ill, are you?"

In spite of her stepbrother's irritation, Ginny began to breathe a little easier. Stephen had left the door ajar behind him.

It wouldn't have been proper for the two of them to be in Ginny's bedroom alone with the door closed. But it was a nicety Ginny was sure Stephen would have overlooked if he'd been facing a true crisis. If he'd believed she was planning to defy him.

"I'm sorry," Ginny said, not bothering to conceal the way her voice trembled. "I didn't hear you. I was asleep, Stephen. Amanda told me I should rest."

At the mention of his wife's name, the angry color faded from Stephen Banks's face, though it was still plain he wasn't happy about the fact that Ginny was still in bed. Equally plain, however, was the fact that, like his wife, Stephen was afraid of pushing Ginny too far.

Ginny pulled in a deep, calming breath. Her brother hadn't discovered what she'd planned. He was merely concerned because she might not be able to see Jack Lawton that evening, just as Amanda had been.

"Amanda did say you might not be feeling well," Stephen admitted. He crossed the room with quick strides to stand beside Ginny's bed. "She also said if you fell ill, you'd have no one but yourself to blame."

Once more, Ginny found herself battling back desperate laughter. It seemed neither Stephen nor Amanda could refrain from criticizing her, in spite of their fear of alienating her.

"What on earth possessed you to open a window in this weather, I'd like to know," Stephen continued.

Oh, no you wouldn't, Stephen, Ginny thought, still struggling to hold in laughter. "I said I was sorry," she protested, clutching the covers to her chin. Out of the corner of her eye, she caught sight of her mother's ring. Ginny eased her right hand down beneath the quilt.

"Well," Stephen Banks murmured, dismissing Ginny's apology with a single syllable.

Without warning, he leaned over to capture her left hand where it still clutched the top of the quilt. He pulled her arm out from under the covers and pressed two fingers against her wrist. Ginny's heart was beating so fast it all but choked her. As he felt her pulse's frantic scramble, Stephen's frown reappeared.

"Hmm," he said through pursed lips. He released Ginny's wrist to press one palm to her forehead. It was all Ginny could do not to flinch. But suddenly, she realized how incredibly warm she was under the winter bed quilt made of wool, with her heaviest coat concealed beneath it. Surely, that would work to her advantage.

"Well, your pulse is fast," Stephen admitted, "and you do feel a little warm." He spun away and took a quick turn about the room, his jerky steps betraying his inner agitation. "You do remember that Jack is expected for dinner this evening," he finally rapped out.

"Of course I remember," Ginny said, as she felt her heart beats begin to slow. *Why did it take me so long to see him as he truly is?* she wondered. Callous. Shallow. Self-obsessed. Neither Stephen nor Amanda had expressed any genuine concern for Ginny's health. She could contract a serious illness, for all they cared. But not before she was safely married to Jack Lawton.

"I'm sure if I just splashed a little cold water on my face—"

"That's a good idea," Stephen seconded at once, swinging around to face her. "In fact, now that I think of it, it might be to our advantage if, for once, you didn't look your best. It wouldn't hurt for you to appear a little frail for a change you know, Ginny. I've always said you were far too robust. Men don't care for a woman who's too strong. It's important for a woman to make a man feel needed."

In spite of the warmth of the covers, Ginny shivered. Did Jack feel the same way her brother did? Was what he wanted not a person, but an ornament? Not that what Jack Lawton wanted mattered anymore. It was what Ginny wanted that mattered now.

How close I came, she thought. *How close to disaster.*

The same distance Stephen was now. But Ginny wasn't about to let herself be sacrificed to her step-brother's schemes. Instead, she would use the impetuosity he so longed to drive out of her to her own advantage.

"If I might have a moment," she said, making a move as if to throw back the quilt, "I'll try to get dressed now, Stephen."

"Of course," Stephen Banks said at once. He moved swiftly to the doorway. "I'll just have Amanda ring for Emily."

"Oh, but—" Ginny began, then caught herself at the last moment. Having to contend with Emily would make her plan for escape even more problematic than it already was, but she'd give away everything if she protested.

The fact that Stephen was willing to have Emily help her dress would usually have been a point in Ginny's favor. Often, Ginny had no one at all. If the occasion was particularly important, Amanda might send her own maid, Miss Scratchard, to help her, a circumstance appreciated by neither.

The older woman's name was the perfect match for her less-than-warm personality, as far as Ginny was concerned, a fact which made her the perfect lady's maid for Amanda.

"Thank you, Stephen," she said. "I'll do my best to be on time."

"Oh, that's all right," Stephen Banks said as he lingered in the doorway, obviously warming to the idea of Ginny's enforced fragility. "I'm sure Jack will understand if you're a little late. It never hurts to make an entrance, you know. Well then, I'll see you at dinner. Don't overdo things now."

With this final bit of advice, he stepped into the hall and pulled the door closed behind him. Ginny continued to lie in bed, counting off the moments until she could be reasonably certain Stephen was at the end of the hall and in his own suite of rooms once more.

One, one thousand. Two, one thousand . . .

Abruptly, she realized she was gripping the quilt so hard her hands ached, biting her lower lip so hard the taste of blood filled her mouth like bitter copper. She threw back the quilt and swung her feet out of bed. She had her coat back on, one hand holding the hat to the top of her head by the time she reached the wardrobe.

Ginny knew she should take a moment to thrust her hatpin through the crown of the hat and into the coil of her own long hair, but she was afraid to take the time to do so, now that absolutely every second counted.

Grasping her heavy carpet bag firmly in one hand, Ginny moved silently to her bedroom door and eased it open. The upstairs hall was empty, silent. Now all she had to do was to make it down the stairs and out the front door before Emily started up the stairs to help her.

The truth was, Ginny had hoped for more time, time enough to get safely to the train station before anyone missed her. The fact that Stephen had summoned a servant to help her dress meant that Ginny's absence would be noticed almost at once. It seemed time was a luxury she'd just have to be prepared to do without.

And I'll have even less of it, she thought, *the longer I stand here hesitating*. She had to go, go *now*, and hope that even the small advantage of surprise she might still have would be enough.

Closing her bedroom door silently behind her, Ginny tiptoed down the hall, her long skirts whispering as she moved rapidly down the staircase. She'd actually reached the bottom and was reaching for the front door when she was pulled up short.

"Why, Miss Ginny!"

Instantly, Ginny whirled around, pressing a desperate finger to her lips. "You didn't see me," she whispered. "Please, Emily."

Emily's blue eyes grew round as teacups as she took in Ginny's appearance. It was plain she wasn't dressed for dinner. Emily's fingers plucked nervously at the front of her apron; her mouth puckered, as if she was trying not to cry.

How young she is, Ginny thought. Emily couldn't be more than fourteen, but she'd been hard at work since before sunup. Her day wouldn't stop until the family had all retired for the night. *My life may become just like hers once I leave here*, Ginny thought.

"But what are you doing? Where are you going, Miss Ginny?" Emily stammered out. "If the master should find out I saw you and then said nothing—"

"It's all right," Ginny said at once, moving away from the front door to lay a hand on Emily's arm. The girl was so frightened she was shivering.

"You don't have to worry about my stepbrother," Ginny said reassuringly. She set down her carpet bag to grasp Emily by both shoulders. "He won't find out. We're all alone. No one can see us or overhear us, Emily."

She watched as the young servant drew a deep, quavering breath. Slowly the shivering stopped.

"What do you want me to do, miss?" Emily asked.

Ginny felt relief spiral through her, though she knew she couldn't feel safe just yet. She was still a long way from the train depot.

"Just go on upstairs to my room. When you see I'm not there, raise the alarm just the way you normally would have. My stepbrother will be so angry with me, he won't have time to think about you. Just don't try and stop me from going. That's all I ask, Emily."

If possible, Emily's eyes grew even rounder. Now, Ginny could plainly see they were filled with tears. "But where will you go? What will you do?" the young servant whispered.

They were good questions, Ginny thought. The same ones she'd been asking herself since yesterday evening, almost endlessly. The fact that she still didn't have good answers didn't mean she could afford to stop her plans now.

"I don't know," she answered honestly. "I only know I can't stay here, Emily. I don't belong here. Can you understand that?"

The young girl nodded, swallowing back her tears. "I think so," she answered slowly. "The master and his wife, they don't care for anyone except themselves."

When she realized what she'd said, she blushed scarlet to the roots of her fine, blond hair. On impulse, Ginny threw her arms around her.

"You *do* understand. Bless you, Emily. Go upstairs, now, and don't look back. I'll be gone before you know it."

Emily straightened her shoulders. "All right," she said, giving her eyes a quick dab with the edge of her apron. "I'll do it. You've always been kind to me—to all of us. I guess this is the way I can return the favor. Just—please—be careful, miss."

"I will," Ginny promised, surprised to find her own throat thick with tears. "And I won't forget you, Emily."

She picked up her carpet bag, walked swiftly to the front door, twisted the knob and pulled it open. She could feel how cold the wind was, even from inside the house.

Clamping her teeth down on the sudden urge to shiver, Ginny stepped out onto the front step. But, as she turned to close the door, a sudden gust of wind struck her. Her unpinned hat sailed from her head. Instinctively, she spun around, grabbing for it.

The front door slipped from her grasp, and slammed shut behind her.

❦ 3 ❧

Instantly, Ginny abandoned any thought of retrieving her hat. Instead, she turned and moved quickly down the steps. Once on the sidewalk, she turned right and headed for the nearest streetcorner as fast as the snowstorm would allow her.

But away from the shelter of the house, the wind struck her full in the face, so strong it threatened to push her right straight back to her stepbrother's doorstep.

At any moment, Ginny expected to hear Stephen's voice cry out, feel his strong arms grab her from behind and hold her. *Don't think about what might be behind you,* she told herself. *Just look straight ahead. Keep on going.*

But when she looked ahead, all she saw was a swirling mass of white, the snowstorm all around her.

Without her hat to protect her head, snow embedded itself in Ginny's hair, stung against her face, insinuated itself inside the collar of her coat as she bent over double. It crunched like gritty sand beneath her feet, but underneath the snow, the sidewalk was slick and icy.

Move! she told herself. *Don't look back.* But every step was a struggle.

The air was so cold Ginny's breath burned in her lungs. The wind in her face made her eyes water. Familiar landmarks disappeared in the swirling snow. It seemed to Ginny as if she were moving in slow motion. Her instincts screamed at her to gather up her skirts and run. Only one small portion of her mind, still clear and calm, urged her to use caution.

If Ginny slipped and fell, she could sprain an ankle or break a leg. If she became injured, she'd have no hope of ever reaching the train depot.

The back of Ginny's neck crawled, as if she could already feel Stephen's eyes upon her. She clenched her teeth against the cold, pulled the collar of her coat up around her neck, and continued her slow progress forward. It wasn't that far to the nearest corner.

You can do this, she told herself fiercely. *You have no choice. All you have to do is put one foot in front of the other.* Without warning, her right foot extended into open space. Ginny jerked it back so quickly she almost tumbled over backward. At last! She'd reached the corner.

But instead of feeling triumphant, she felt her heart plummet in dismay. The snow was falling so thick and fast, Ginny couldn't see across the street. How on earth would she be able to hail a hansom?

According to her plan, all Ginny'd had to do was leave the house and walk around the nearest streetcorner. Once out of sight of Stephen and Amanda's bedroom window, she'd counted on at least a small margin of safety, and quick access to transportation.

It was easy to hail the horse and buggies known as hansom cabs in the Banks's prosperous neighborhood. Only the most wealthy families continued to keep their own horses and carriages, and the streetcar didn't run through the area yet. The easy availability of transportation had been a key part of Ginny's plan to escape.

But, from the moment she'd set foot outside the house, all her desperately laid plans had been swept away, blown off course by the driving wind of the snowstorm.

"Ginny! Virginia Nolan!"

Ginny's heart leaped in her chest. That was Stephen's voice! The slam of the front door had made her worst nightmare come true. He'd discovered she was missing before she could put any more than half a block between them.

Her only hope now lay in the fact that Stephen didn't know which way she'd gone after leaving the house. If he set off in the wrong direction ...

But if Stephen guessed right, he could reach her within minutes. And the longer she hesitated, the more she increased her stepbrother's chances of locating her.

There's nothing for it, Ginny thought. Praying that the accumulation of snow would cushion her fall, she gathered her skirts in one hand, tightened her grip on her carpet bag with the other, and jumped into the street.

She landed in a snowbank clear up to her knees.

The cold was so intense, Ginny bit down on her tongue to keep from crying out. She could feel the snow, soaking through her skirts and petticoats in spite of her attempt to hold them up and out of the way. Her feet were so cold she could barely feel her toes.

"Dammit, Ginny! I know you're out here somewhere! You'll never get away with this, you know. Now, answer me!"

Ginny's stomach clenched. She began to shiver, uncontrollably. But she didn't think the cold had brought on the trembling. She was sure it was the sound of her stepbrother's voice. Even through the call of the wind, Ginny could hear the sound of Stephen's fury.

Was he closer than he'd been before? *No!* she thought. *I can't let him catch me.* If he did, Ginny was sure her life wouldn't be worth living. Once back under Stephen's "protection," she'd be a prisoner forever. Her life would be unthinkable.

That isn't going to happen, she thought. *Not if I have to walk all the way to the train depot.* Still clutching her carpet bag in one hand, holding the other in front of her like a child making its way down a long, dark hallway, Ginny waded out into the street.

She'd only taken half a dozen steps when she thought she heard the jingle of a horse's harness. She spun in the direction of the sound. Her feet slipped from under her. Ginny fell painfully to her hands and knees.

Without warning, a shape loomed out of the snow above her. With a cry, Ginny threw herself to one side. *Oh, God,* she thought. *I've given myself away.*

She heard a shout, and prayed that it was the driver of the carriage, not her stepbrother. A moment later, she heard the voice again.

"Is there someone down there?"

Desperately, Ginny pushed herself to her feet. "I need a ride," she called out. "I need to get to the train depot. Is this a cab? Can you take me?"

"I can," the driver shouted. "But it's slow going, I should warn you."

"It doesn't matter," Ginny called back. If she missed the train to Seattle, she'd wait as long as it took for the next train—the next train to anywhere. All she wanted was to get away from her step-brother. *Just get me away from here.*

"Can you get in on your own?" the driver called down. "I don't want to let go of the horse in all this wind."

"I think so," Ginny said. She felt her way along the side of the coach until her fingers encountered the door handle. She pushed it down, pulled the door open, hiked her skirts up as best she could, and put her foot on the first step, praying it wouldn't slip right off. The first step of a hansom was about a foot and a half off the ground. Getting into the cabs was difficult even in the best conditions, and conditions could hardly be considered to be the best right now.

"Ginny!" she heard Stephen shout once more. This time, she was almost certain that the sound was closer. She didn't know whether he could actually see her yet or not. But as soon as he could, she was sure he would try to stop her.

With all her strength, Ginny heaved her carpet bag into the hansom, pulled herself up onto the seat, and slammed the door behind her.

"Go!" she shouted to the driver. "Please, go now."

In the next instant, she was jerked against the back of the seat as the horse started forward. She swore she heard one final shout, just as the hansom turned a corner.

Ginny sat in the cold, dark interior of the coach. After a few moments, she pulled her carpet bag across the seat and onto her lap, hugging it to her chest as if it were a long-lost lover.

I did it, she thought. She'd escaped from Stephen, and she was safe—for the time being.

But if Stephen had overheard her shouted instructions to the hansom driver, Ginny knew her safety would be all too short-lived. Even now, her stepbrother would be trying to find transportation of his own, hoping to intercept her at the train depot.

Even if Stephen hadn't overheard her, the chances were good he still might find her. If Ginny truly wished to get away, there were only so many places she could go.

Please, she prayed as her fingers found the surface of her mother's cameo. *Let my luck change for the better. Don't let Stephen catch me. I don't want to end up like a bird in a gilded cage.*

All the way across town as she shivered in the dark, Ginny prayed that she would be in time to board the train that would take her across the mountains to safety in Seattle.

❧ 4 ❧

By the time Ginny reached the train depot she felt all but frozen.

Her fingers had cramped from her tight grip on her carpet bag. Beneath her cold, soaked skirts, her legs and feet had tingled painfully and then gone numb. She'd tried stamping against the floor of the cab to keep the blood flowing, but she wasn't sure how well it had worked.

That would be a fine mess, she thought. To finally reach the depot, then be unable to board.

The trip to the depot seemed to take forever. As it progressed, Ginny began to feel as if she was encased in some strange, otherworldly cocoon. Though protected from the wind, the interior of the hansom was still cold and dark. The only sounds Ginny could hear were her own heart beats, her own harsh breaths, and the wail of the wind above them both.

When the hansom finally slowed and stopped, Ginny almost didn't notice it at first, as if the motion of the cab through the long, cold journey had left her mesmerized. It wasn't until the driver opened the panel in the roof that he used to communicate with passengers that Ginny realized they had stopped.

"Here's the train depot," the driver called down. "The train's still out in front. Looks like you're in luck."

Ginny felt a sudden flush of heat rush through her as she realized she could hear a new sound. Slicing through the roar of the wind came the deep hiss of some enormous beast: the sound of the steam locomotive, primed and ready to go.

A burst of elation shot through Ginny so abruptly she felt dizzy. She had done it. She'd made it to the train depot. In spite of Stephen's pursuit. In spite of the storm. All she had to do now was board, and the train would do the rest. It would carry her to safety, far away from the false life her stepbrother had planned for her.

Ginny flexed her fingers and gave her feet one last stomp against the floor of the hansom. Then she leaned over and opened the door. The wind caught it at once, slamming it back against the body of the cab, but for the first time since she'd set out in it, Ginny didn't mind the fury of the storm. She'd reached her destination. The storm couldn't hurt her any longer.

Quickly now, desperately eager to reach the train, she slid along the seat toward the open door and prepared to jump down. But just as she was about to set her foot upon the step, the cab driver materialized below her.

He was muffled in a greatcoat, the collar turned up around his chin. He had a scarf wound around his neck, and a cap pulled down over his ears, almost to his eyebrows. The only part of his face Ginny could see were his raw, red cheeks, and a pair of sparkling blue eyes.

"Toss me your bag," the cab driver said. "I reckon you're pretty cold and stiff by now. You'll need some help getting down after that long ride. The horse can stand here. There's some cover. Besides, the snow has stopped."

Ginny looked, and was surprised to see that he was right. During her endless journey to the train depot the snow had stopped. But the wind still blew, fierce and bone-chilling.

Grateful for the driver's offer of assistance, Ginny tossed the carpet bag down. He caught it, set it on the ground, then reached toward her. Ginny placed her foot on the step, then tumbled out into his arms.

"There now," the driver said. "What did I tell

you? Just stand still a minute, miss, till your legs remember what God made them for. They'll likely hurt a bit. What do they call it?"

"Pins and needles," Ginny answered. And they'd just appeared in full force. After what felt like hours of being numb, the feeling was returning to her legs with a vengeance.

"Stamp 'em," the driver said. "That'll get the blood going."

Ginny stamped her feet, hearing the snow crunch beneath them. She gritted her teeth as the pain shot upward, making her legs wobble. She was grateful for the support of the cab driver's arms. Without him, Ginny was sure she'd have tumbled right into the snow. She put her hands on his shoulders and stamped with all her might, determined to get the strength back into her legs as quickly as possible.

If Amanda could see this, she'd have an absolute fit, Ginny thought. But then everything about this situation would give Amanda fits. At the thought of her stepsister-in-law, Ginny looked around. If Stephen had figured out where she'd gone, the break in the weather would work in his favor, not hers. She had to get onto the train as soon as possible. Fortunately, the cab driver had brought her right up to the train. Since it was in front of the station, it was actually between Ginny and the depot.

"Thank you," she said to the driver. "I feel much better now. How much do I owe you?"

He released her at once and stepped back, all business. "That'll be fifty cents, ma'am," he said. Ginny dug in one coat pocket and produced a handful of change. She pressed it into the driver's outstretched hand. Then she picked up her carpet bag and began to move around the back of the cab toward the train.

"Wait a minute," the driver called after her. "You've given me way too much."

Ginny turned back, a genuine smile lighting her face for the first time since the night before. She hadn't truly smiled once since she'd overheard the conversation between Stephen and Amanda.

"No, I haven't," she said. For what he'd given her, the chance at freedom, no price was too high. Ginny would have handed over her last cent, if that's what it took. "Consider it a bonus, because of the weather," she went on. "I'd never have made it to the station without you."

"Well, then," the cab driver said, giving the bill of his cap a tug. "I'm much obliged to you, ma'am. Good luck and safe journey."

Ginny smiled once again. She knew he was simply being polite, but the sentiment still warmed her. She was definitely going to need all the luck and good wishes she could get.

"Thank you," she answered.

The driver touched his cap once more, swung himself up onto his seat, then chirruped to the horse and started the cab moving forward. As it pulled away, Ginny caught her breath.

The train sat in front of the station like a great black dragon. At its head, a thick vapor of part steam, part coal smoke oozing from its smokestack, was the great, jet-black locomotive. Behind it, lining up like beads along a string, Ginny counted seven cars. The one on the very end, she knew, would be an observation car, or "smoker."

Here male passengers would be allowed to smoke, and drink, if they'd brought spirits with them. But Ginny didn't think anyone would be standing outside on the back observation platform to view the passing scenery on this trip. It was too likely they'd be all but frozen.

In the cars directly behind the locomotive, Ginny could see mail and baggage being loaded. Farther down the train, she saw faces peering from windows, and decided those must be the passenger coaches. She wondered which one would have a place for her.

You'll never find out if you just stand here, she told herself. *You'd better get going.*

Even as she moved forward, two sharp whistles split the air. "Board!" she heard a voice shouting.

Another five minutes, and she'd have missed the train. Ginny moved quickly toward the nearest coach.

"I don't have a ticket!" she called out to the conductor.

"That's all right, ma'am," he said, turning toward her. He gestured with one hand, urging her forward. "Get on board and we can settle up once we're underway. Just hurry up, now. We're about to get going." He put a hand under her elbow and helped her step up into the train.

"Ginny!" a voice behind her shouted.

Ginny's heart and footsteps faltered. Stephen had found her! But she didn't look back, knew she couldn't acknowledge Stephen's shout in any way. If she did, she'd alert her fellow passengers that she was the one for whom he was crying out.

And she'd acknowledge that he had power over her.

Instead, she began to move swiftly down the length of the train car.

"Ginny," she heard Stephen's voice cry again. "Don't let that young woman board the train," he went on. "Stop her!"

Ginny's eyes darted right and left. If she could just find some place to conceal herself . . . *I can't give up now. Not when I've come so far. I can't let Stephen stop me.*

But the farther she progressed along the car, the more Ginny felt her hope falter. Nowhere did she see a place where she might hide. There was only row after row of straight-backed seats, all facing toward her.

I'm in a day coach, she thought. The kind used for short excursions. But surely a train such as this would have more than just day coaches. The trip to Seattle required an overnight journey. The train must also include sleeping accommodations. If Ginny could reach a sleeper car, she might hide in one of the berths.

She reached the end of the car, pulled the connecting door open, just as she heard Stephen's voice, arguing with the conductor.

"No, I don't intend to travel on this contraption! My sister is on this train without my permission. What I intend to do is stop her!"

Ginny pulled the door closed behind her. She maneuvered through the small covered area that connected the day coach with the car behind it. Pulling the second door open, she felt a tiny spurt of relief.

It was a sleeper. Now all she had to do was to pray the conductor delayed Stephen long enough for Ginny to locate a place to conceal herself. And then, she had to pray that Stephen never found her.

Ginny moved down the aisle as quickly as she

could, often turning sideways to avoid colliding with her fellow passengers. All around her, people were preparing to retire for the night. Like the day car, the sleeping car had no individual compartments. It was open. To convert the car into its sleeping accommodations, lower berths were formed by pulling special extensions out between the seats. Upper berths, all but invisible when folded up during the day, were pulled down into an open position.

A porter bustled near the front of the car, making up berths, helping a woman settle two small children. He stepped aside to let Ginny pass with hardly a glance in her direction.

"I saw her come this way, I tell you!"

Ginny picked up her pace. It took every ounce of willpower she had not to glance back over her shoulder. If she once looked at Stephen, all would be lost. Never had she heard her stepbrother's voice so filled with fury, though it sounded strange and muffled.

He must be between the cars, Ginny thought. If he entered the sleeper and saw her . . .

"No," she whispered, completely unaware she'd voiced her desperate thought aloud. She'd all but reached the end of the car. Should she continue on to the next one, or stop now, search for a place to hide? "Please, God, don't let him catch me."

"There," a voice said. "Up there."

Ginny skidded to a stop. A girl about her own age was standing at the end of the car. Ginny had a brief impression of startled hazel eyes staring straight into hers for a fraction of a second, then warming for a reason Ginny couldn't fathom.

"It's all right," the girl said. "Just give me your hand."

Ginny reached out, and felt ice cold fingers close around hers. *She's as afraid as I am.* But of what, Ginny didn't know.

"Go on," the girl said. "Climb up."

Without stopping to think any longer, Ginny stepped onto the lower berth and tossed her carpet bag upward. The girl gave her a boost. A moment later, Ginny was sliding into the upper berth. Her unknown friend yanked the green drapes that provided privacy for each set of berths closed behind her. But she stayed close. Ginny could see the impression of her back where it pressed against the curtain.

"She's in here, I tell you. Dammit, Ginny, I demand you show yourself this instant!" Stephen's voice bellowed.

Just in time, Ginny thought. It was all she could do not to clap her hands over her ears to shut out the sound of Stephen's voice. But she was afraid any movement she made might disturb the curtain protecting her hiding place.

She forced herself to lie absolutely still, and heard a ripple of consternation pass through the sleeping car. Stephen had done something no gentleman ever did: he'd cursed in mixed company.

"Can I help you, sir?" she heard the porter ask. "Though I'm afraid I'll have to ask you to remember there are women and children in this car."

"I'm not blind. I can see that," Ginny heard Stephen snap back. She was sure it galled him to be chastised by a porter, someone he'd consider no better than one of his own household servants.

"May I help you, sir?" the porter asked again.

"I'm looking for my sister. I'm her guardian, and she has boarded this train without my consent. I'm certain she came into this car. I demand that you turn her over to me this instant!"

There was something in Stephen's voice that Ginny had never heard before. Something more than anger. This was something ugly, something brutal.

She tried not to think of what would happen to her if he caught her now, now that she'd forced him to follow her through the storm. Been the cause of him being taken to task for his behavior in public. She felt a hard knot of fear form in the center of her stomach.

"All right, Lucius," she heard another man's voice say. Ginny thought she recognized the voice of the conductor who'd helped her board earlier. "Folks in the day car remember seeing a young woman come through in a hurry. It may be she came this way. Do you remember seeing anyone come through here?"

Ginny felt the knot twist. She held her breath.

"No, sir," the porter answered. "I can't say that I did. But I have been pretty busy in here."

"Oh, this is ridiculous," Stephen burst out impatiently. "I can't believe the railroad is so mismanaged. I tell you she must be here somewhere."

"What's your sister's name, sir?" Ginny heard the porter, Lucius, ask.

"Virginia," Stephen snapped.

"Excuse me, ladies and gentlemen," the porter called out, "but is there a young lady named Virginia anywhere in this car?"

"Virginia!" exclaimed a voice so close to Ginny that in spite of her desire to stay motionless, she flinched back.

It was the voice of the girl who'd helped her into her hiding place. She was still standing right on the other side of the green curtain that formed the only barrier between Ginny and Stephen.

"Virginia," the girl repeated, the surprise plain in her voice. "But that's my name!"

❦ 5 ❦

Ginny felt her heart freeze inside her chest. *No!* she thought. *This can't be happening!*

Had the girl tricked her into hiding so that she could reveal her to her stepbrother? *But I've never seen her in my life before*, Ginny thought. Such a plan just didn't make sense.

"Did you say your name was Virginia?" Ginny heard the conductor ask.

Ginny pressed herself against the back of the berth, clutching her carpet bag to her chest, trying to put as much distance as possible between herself and the green curtain. But even as she did it, she realized the gesture was useless. If the young woman revealed where Ginny was, nothing in the world would stop Stephen from finding her.

"Yes, my name is Virginia," the young woman said.

"Will you come forward, please, miss?" Ginny heard the conductor ask.

Ginny heard the whisper of skirts, the click of shoes as the girl who'd helped conceal her moved off down the aisle. The green curtain in front of Ginny's face swayed ever so slightly as the girl stepped forward. Ginny held her breath.

"Now then," she heard the conductor say after a moment. "Is this the young lady you're looking for?"

"What is the meaning of this?" Stephen's voice said, his tone harsh.

"You have asked if there is a young woman named Virginia in the car," the conductor answered in a strained but patient voice. "This is the only young woman who has come forward. I take it she is not your sister?"

But when Stephen spoke again, Ginny knew at once that he'd completely ignored the conductor, speaking instead to her unknown friend in a voice that made goosebumps rise on Ginny's skin.

"You're trying to trick me, aren't you?" Stephen asked. "The two of you are in this thing together. Where is she? What have you done?"

Without warning, the girl named Virginia gave a sharp exclamation. "Let go of me," she cried out. "Let go, you're hurting my arm."

"*That's enough!*" the conductor said, all his patience vanishing. Ginny heard a child begin to whimper, the sound quickly hushed. "Sir, your behavior is inexcusable," the conductor went on. "I'm afraid I must ask you to leave this train at once."

"I tell you, I will not," Stephen snapped back. "I will stay here until I find my sister. I demand to know what's going on."

"*No.*" The conductor's voice was as hard and quick as the crack of a whip.

"Sir," he said forcefully. "No one on this car has anything to tell you. You have laid rough hands on this young lady for no other reason than that she is not your sister. Your behavior is inexcusable, and it is dangerous. I order you to leave this train at once. If you do not go of your own accord, I will summon assistance and have you thrown off."

Ginny heard Stephen make a choking sound. "Mr. Hill will hear of this," he rapped out. "I am not without influence."

Absolute silence descended upon the sleeping car. Ginny pressed one fist against her mouth.

James Hill was one of the most powerful men in all of Washington. People called him the Empire Builder. He was the force behind the Great Northern Railway. A word from Hill, and the conductor could be fired and never allowed to work for the railroad again.

Maybe I should give myself up, Ginny thought. *I'm putting other people in danger, innocent people.*

"Naturally, you must do as you think fit, sir," the conductor said in a stiff voice. "As must I. My first duty is to the safety of these passsengers, and I believe you are a menace to that safety. You will leave this train. *Now*."

In the split second of silence that followed, Ginny could hear someone breathing harshly through his mouth. *Stephen*, she thought. She didn't think anyone had ever spoken to her stepbrother in so forceful a manner.

"You'll be sorry," Stephen said, his voice all but a snarl. *He sounds like an animal*, Ginny thought. A predator furious at being deprived of its prey. "You haven't heard the end of this, I promise you."

She heard heavy footsteps, then the bang of a door. There was another moment of complete silence. Then, slowly, Ginny began to hear the rustling of garments and bedding that told her the other occupants of the sleeping car were trying to return to normal.

"We'll be getting under way in just a few moments, ladies and gentlemen," the conductor said, his voice sounding tired. "I apologize for this distressing interruption."

"If he does go to Hill, I'll speak for you," said a man's voice. "I'm not without some influence myself. Here's my card."

"Judge McAllister, thank you, sir," the conductor

answered, his voice warming. "If you will all excuse me now, I must see to the rest of the cars. If you need anything, please ask Lucius to assist you."

Again, Ginny heard the sound of footsteps, this time followed by the gentle but firm closing of the coach door. Ginny could all but hear her fellow passengers catching their collective breaths.

"When is the train going to start moving, Mama?" a plaintive young voice inquired.

"The conductor said it wouldn't be long now," a woman replied. "Come on now, let's get you settled in for the night."

"Can I sleep on top?" the child asked, the tone excited.

"No," his mother answered, a laugh in her own. "You most certainly may not. The restless way you sleep, you'll fall off in the middle of the night."

"But I could fall from the bottom, too," the child protested.

"Well," his mother said practically. "At least you won't have so far to go."

Ginny felt rather than heard the return of the young woman who'd helped conceal her. The curtains which veiled her hiding place stirred ever so slightly but did not part.

"Are you all right, ma'am?" Ginny heard the porter, Lucius, inquire, his voice right by her head.

"I'm fine," the girl named Virginia replied in a

subdued voice. "He frightened me, but he didn't hurt me. Though I must say," she went on, her tone rallying, "I was never so glad *not* to be somebody's sister in my whole life."

"Wherever that girl is, I hope he never finds her," Ginny heard the woman with the young child comment. Relief made hot tears prick at the back of Ginny's eyes. Without warning, she heard two whistles sounding long and mournful through the icy night.

"There we go," the porter called out. "We'll be under way in just a moment. Does anybody need my help?"

Ginny heard his heavy footsteps, moving off toward the front of the sleeping car. She lay perfectly still, breathing softly through her mouth, listening to her heart pound. Where was Virginia? Was she still right beside the berth?

In the next instant, Ginny almost tumbled out as the train jerked forward. Slowly at first, then with ever increasing speed, Great Northern #25 began to glide out of the Spokane depot.

I've done it, Ginny thought. *I'm actually getting away.*

Soon, the life she'd lived with Stephen and Amanda would be far behind. She'd leave behind the suitor they'd chosen, who'd never really loved her. Even the graves of her parents would be left behind. All the external things that had made her Virginia Nolan.

Who will I be now? Ginny wondered. How would she change, now that she could choose for herself?

As if watching her new life revealed on a stage, Ginny saw the green curtain screening the berth pull back. Slowly, the form of the girl who'd hidden her came into view, silhouetted against the darkening windows of the berth just opposite. Ginny couldn't see her face clearly, just her outline.

"You can come out now. It's safe," the girl named Virginia murmured.

～6～

In total silence, Ginny scooted forward. Virginia reached to take the carpet bag, then dropped it to the floor. Ginny swung her legs out over the edge of the upper berth, twisting over onto her stomach. She felt Virginia's hand guide one leg to a toe hold on the lower berth. Ginny put her weight down on it. A moment later, she had both feet on the wooden floor.

Slowly, Ginny turned toward the girl who'd so unexpectedly saved her from her stepbrother. As she got her first good look at Virginia's face, Ginny's breath caught in her throat. For a moment, she felt dizzy, disoriented.

Looking at Virginia was almost like looking into a mirror. She looked just like her.

The match wasn't exact, it was true, but the other girl had the same dark hair, the same fine, porcelain-pale skin, though her hazel eyes were just a shade or two lighter than Ginny's dark brown ones.

She was a little shorter, too, Ginny realized. She could see the other passengers in the sleeping car by looking over Virginia's shoulder. But still, they looked so much alike they could have been taken for sisters.

No wonder Stephen had been so angry, she thought. He'd been so sure he'd caught her. Virginia's resemblance to Ginny must have seemed a cruel and bitter trick.

"Is your name really Virginia?" she blurted out.

A quick smile flitted across the other girl's features. "Yes, it really is. Virginia Hightower."

"I'm Virginia Nolan," Ginny answered. The other girl said nothing else, though she did continue to regard Ginny steadily, almost expectantly, as if she was waiting for something. What it was, Ginny couldn't tell.

Suddenly uncomfortable, she found herself saying the first thing that came to mind to fill the silence.

"My mother wanted to call me that, after her own mother. But Papa always said Virginia was too long a name for me. I was always dashing from place to place, all those syllables would never catch up. So he called me Ginny instead."

"Ginny," the other girl repeated. "A nickname. I

like that. My papa never called me anything if he could help it." There was another awkward pause. "Is that horrible man really your stepbrother?" Virginia burst out.

All of a sudden, Ginny felt exhausted. She sat down hard on the lower berth. After a moment, Virginia sat down beside her. When they turned to face one another, tucking their feet up onto the berth, the two girls were all but hidden from view.

"Yes, he is my stepbrother," Ginny said. "My guardian."

"Oh, but, I thought you said—" Virginia broke off, her face turning bright red. "I'm sorry," she said. "I don't mean to pry."

"It's all right," Ginny said. "You can ask me. What?"

"I thought you said—" Virginia stammered again.

She's shy, Ginny realized suddenly. So shy Virginia was actually wringing her hands in distress. *How on earth had she ever had the courage to stand up to Stephen?* Ginny wondered. *Even I could barely find the courage to do that.*

"I mean—you mentioned your father—"

Without warning, the tears Ginny had fought back earlier filled her eyes. She blinked rapidly to keep them from spilling over.

"My father is dead," she answered softly. "Not

quite two years now. He died on his honeymoon, about a week after he married Stephen's mother. After Papa died, Stephen and his wife were the only relations I had left. They didn't want to take me in, but they didn't have a choice."

And neither did I, she thought. *Until last night.* Then, she'd taken the only choice she could see, no matter what the consequences.

Virginia's hands stilled. "So your father was a good man," she said. "And you weren't happy living among strangers." Her voice was calm, but Ginny could hear the fine tremor of fear running through it.

"No, I wasn't," she answered honestly. "But I don't think it was because they were strangers. I think it was just because of—who they were. And who I was. They didn't want me, you see. No matter what I did."

"Yes, I see," Virginia said softly. "But, if someone really wanted you, you think it might be all right, even if you didn't know them very well to begin with?" she prompted.

Ginny stared across the berth. Virginia's face looked hopeful, even eager. But, as Ginny looked more closely, she could see the rapid rise and fall of Virginia's chest. Her hazel eyes glittered, almost as if she had a fever.

She's desperate, Ginny thought. *As desperate as I was.*

"If someone really wanted you, I imagine almost anything might be all right," Ginny answered slowly.

Across the berth, Virginia Hightower looked back down at her hands. "I hope so," she said softly.

"Thank you," Ginny said.

Virginia looked back up. "What for?"

In spite of the seriousness of their conversation, Ginny gave a helpless spurt of laughter. How could it be that Virginia didn't know what for?

"For hiding me from my stepbrother," she said. "If it hadn't been for you—"

"Why did you run away?" Virginia suddenly asked.

This has to be the strangest conversation I've ever had in my life, Ginny thought. Never had she shared such confidences. But then, she'd never had anyone to share them with. After her father's death, there'd been no one who cared.

"I discovered something—unpleasant—about my stepbrother," Ginny said. "I discovered he'd been stealing the inheritance my mother left to me. To cover it up he—"

At the thought of Jack Lawton, Ginny felt her heart cinch. "He encouraged me to believe that one of his friends was in love with me," she finished in a rush. "Stephen wanted me to marry Jack. I think he even would have forced me."

"Because once you were married to his friend, your stepbrother would have been safe," Virginia filled in.

Ginny nodded. Virginia might be shy, but that didn't mean she was stupid. "Why did you help me?" Ginny asked.

Virginia's pale skin flushed. Once again, her hands worried one another in her lap. On impulse, Ginny reached with both of her own to cover them.

"It's all right," she said. "You don't have to answer if it makes you upset. I just want you to know how much I appreciate what you did. If there's anything I can ever do for you—"

"It was the look on your face," Virginia interrupted.

Whatever answer Ginny had expected, it certainly wasn't this. "The look on my face?" she said.

Now it was Virginia's turn to nod. "You looked so frightened, so—desperate. It was just the way I felt inside and so—"

"Don't tell me you're on this train because you're running away, too!" Ginny broke in.

Virginia gave a reluctant breath of laughter. But she turned her hands over, so that her fingers clutched at Ginny's. Looking into the soft hazel of the other girl's eyes, Ginny could suddenly see the desperation in them was back. The hunted look had disappeared while Virginia had listened to Ginny tell her story. But now that she was speaking of herself, it had returned with a vengeance.

"No," Virginia said softly. "I'm not running away. Just the opposite, in fact. I suppose you could say I'm running toward.

"I'm going to Seattle to be married."

✺ 7 ✺

"Congratulations!" Ginny cried, knowing it was the wrong thing to say even as she heard herself say it. Being engaged wasn't always cause for celebration, as she herself knew all too well. "What's his name?"

"His name is Nicholas Bennett," Virginia said in so low a voice Ginny had to lean forward to hear it. "My father arranged the marriage just before he died."

"Well," Ginny said. Perhaps if she kept talking long enough, she could discover the cause behind the hunted look in Virginia Hightower's eyes. "What does he look like? How did you meet? Tell me all about him."

"I don't know," Virginia said, in a voice so low Ginny wasn't certain that she'd heard her correctly.

"You don't *know?*"

Virginia shook her head. "I've never seen him,"

she explained, her voice a whisper. "All I know is that he's the son of my father's dearest childhood friend. Papa and Mr. Bennett—the elder Mr. Bennett, I mean—they grew up together. The Bennetts stayed in Seattle, but Papa came east. He arranged the marriage just before he died. He made me promise—on his deathbed—"

"Wait a minute," Ginny exclaimed, her head reeling. Surely such things didn't happen anymore, did they? This was the twentieth century, after all. "You're on your way to marry a man you've never even *met?*"

Mutely, Virginia nodded.

"Well, no wonder you're so desperate."

Ginny released Virginia's hands to clap a hand over her mouth. Her impetuosity had carried her away again. "I'm sorry," she said. "That was thoughtless of me. I shouldn't have said it."

"Why not? It's true," Virginia said. "Didn't I say I thought you looked as desperate as I felt?"

"You did," Ginny admitted. She stared at Virginia, sitting motionless on the far side of the berth. "No wonder you were so worried about strangers," she added softly. "But isn't there anyone else you could go to? What about your mother's family?"

Virginia shook her head. "If only I could meet Nicholas first," she suddenly burst out. "Learn what he's like before I marry him. But there's no time—

no time at all. He's meeting the train in Seattle and we're to be married within the week. I don't even know how he feels about it. What if he's angry? What if he hates me?"

Once again, Ginny reached for Virginia's hands. Her heart went out to her. At least she'd known Jack Lawton. *But you didn't really, did you?* her mind asked. All she'd truly seen of Jack was what he'd wished to show her.

How did you truly come to know someone, to trust them, Ginny wondered. How did a total stranger become transformed into a friend, a lover, a husband?

"I'm sorry," she said. "I wish that there was something I could do to help."

"Well, now, what have we here?" said a voice beside her. Ginny jumped, starting so hard her head thumped against the upper berth.

"Mr. Anderson!" Virginia exclaimed. Ginny turned to see the porter standing in the aisle beside them. "This is my friend Ginny," Virginia continued in a rush. "We got on together in Spokane, don't you remember?"

"Well, now," the porter said again, this time more slowly. His dark eyes traveled from one girl to the other. "Can't say as I do," he admitted, even more slowly. Without warning, a smile split his face.

"I can tell you this much, though. I'd have a hard

time telling you two gals apart. Like two peas in a pod, that's what you are." But his eyes finally focused straight on Ginny. "I'm sorry, ma'am," he said. "But what did you say your name was?"

Ginny swallowed past a huge lump in her throat. "Ginny," she said.

Lucius Anderson ran his knuckles against one side of his chin. "Ginny, huh. That'd be short for Virginia, now, generally, wouldn't it?"

Now the lump in Ginny's throat had grown so large she wasn't sure she could force a single syllable out around it. "Generally," she managed, but her voice came out in a croak.

Again, Lucius Anderson looked from one girl to the other. Once more, his eyes stopped on Ginny. "How far you goin'?" he inquired.

"As far as Seattle," Ginny answered. "But I got to the station too late to buy my ticket. The conductor said I could do it once I was on the train—"

Her voice trailed off as she realized what she'd just done: admitted that she and Virginia hadn't boarded the train together. The other girl already had a ticket, and the porter knew it.

Lucius Anderson eased his cap off, then scratched his head. Ginny could practically see his mind working, turning over whether or not to ask her any more questions.

"Had some unpleasantness just before we left the

depot," the porter said at last. "I don't suppose you happened to see any of that?"

"No, I didn't," Ginny answered promptly. "The cold weather made me feel a little unwell, so I lay down as soon as I boarded. I didn't see a thing until after we left Spokane."

At least it's the truth, she thought, relieved that the porter hadn't asked her if she'd *heard* anything before they'd left the depot. Then, as she looked into Lucius Anderson's kind eyes, she had the feeling he knew exactly what she was thinking, and that he'd phrased his question the way he had on purpose.

"So you couldn't be expected to know anything about that business, then," the porter continued.

"No, sir," Ginny replied softly. She looked down at her hands in her lap. Now she was the one who was worrying them back and forth. "I'm sorry, Mr. Anderson," she added after a moment. Her presence on the train could put the porter's job in jeopardy, too, and she was sure that they both knew it.

"Well, now," Lucius Anderson said for the third and final time. He settled the cap back on his head with one brisk gesture, as if he'd come to an important decision.

"No need to apologize for a thing like that, I reckon. Seeing as how it's so late, I'll take care getting your ticket fixed up myself. That way, you can just settle in for a good night's sleep. No need to see the conductor."

Relief swept through Ginny so swiftly she felt light-headed. The porter was sparing her more questions, and more explanations. He wouldn't be the only one to realize that Ginny was a nickname for Virginia. No doubt, so would the conductor.

But if Lucius Anderson handled getting her ticket himself, the conductor would never need to learn her identity. Ginny would be safe all the way to Seattle. She made swift eye contact with Virginia, sitting silently on the far end of the berth. The other girl's mouth turned upward in a slow smile.

"Thank you, Mr. Anderson," Ginny whispered.

"Yes, thank you, Mr. Anderson," Virginia seconded.

Lucius Anderson touched one finger to the brim of his cap. "Don't mention it, young ladies. Now I guess we'd better settle up. You're just going the one way?"

Ginny nodded.

"Then I'll need eight dollars," Lucius Anderson told her.

Ginny reached into her pocket and retrieved the fare, startled to discover she still had her coat on. In the excitement of hiding from Stephen, followed by the revelations during her conversation with Virginia, she'd forgotten to take it off.

Now the sudden realization that she was wearing her coat made Ginny realize something else. Her lace-up ankle boots and stockings, her skirts and petticoats from the knees down were soaked clear through. She'd catch cold for sure if she didn't change them before retiring for the night.

"Anything else you young ladies need?" Lucius Anderson asked.

Ginny brought her mind back to the present with a jerk. "Is there a place where I can change, Mr. Anderson?" she asked. "I got pretty wet coming across town in all the snow."

"There's a ladies' washroom right at the end of the car here," the porter said. "Though some ladies do prefer to change in their berths."

Ginny didn't see how she'd possibly be able to change out of her long skirts and petticoats while lying in her berth, though she could understand why some women might choose to do so.

The sleeping car accommodated both men and women. If a woman changed in the washroom, then walked back to her berth in her nightclothes, there was no telling who might see her. All a man would have to do was pull aside the curtain in front of his berth to get a look. There were even stories of men meeting their mistresses on the sleeper cars, while wives stayed unsuspectingly at home.

Fortunately for Ginny, the washroom was near

the berth Virginia had already chosen. She wouldn't have far to go to reach the washroom. Now that she thought about it, Ginny realized at least one woman had passed by during her conversation with Virginia. But Ginny had been so wrapped up in what she and her new friend were saying, she hadn't paid anyone else any attention.

"Thank you, Mr. Anderson," she said once more.

"Don't mention it," the porter answered. "You young ladies have a good night's sleep, now. We'll be west of the mountains by the time you wake up in the morning. Trip'll be over before you know it."

He turned, and moved back down the aisle. Just before he passed out of earshot, Ginny swore she heard him chuckling, "Just like two peas in a pod."

She glanced across at Virginia to see that she'd heard Lucius, too. "We really do look alike, you know. We could easily be taken for sisters."

Virginia nodded. "I know. I think it's part of what made me want to help you. When I looked at you, it was just like looking at myself."

All of a sudden, Ginny sat bolt upright, hardly noticing when her head bumped the upper berth, the need to change her cold, wet skirts forgotten. She'd just found the perfect way to pay Virginia back for her kindness, and protect herself, too.

"For heaven's sake, what is it?" Virginia exclaimed. "You're not really ill, are you?"

"No," Ginny answered. "But to tell you the truth, I don't feel much like myself."

This might well be the most impetuous thing she'd ever done, even more impetuous than running away. She could practically hear all the syllables that made up her name, frantically running to catch up with her. By the time they got there, Ginny had decided.

"I don't feel like myself at all," she said, unable to suppress a grin. She leaned forward, placing her hands on Virginia's shoulders, bringing her face close to her new friend's.

"As a matter of fact," Ginny Nolan said to Virginia Hightower, "I think I feel like you."

8

Virginia's eyes widened, until the size that Emily's had reached when Ginny had told her she was leaving home was nothing by comparison. Virginia's eyes were the size of dinner plates.

"You feel like me?" she breathed. "You mean—"

Ginny nodded, her eyes still on Virginia's face. "I think we should trade places."

Virginia sat back, and Ginny did likewise. It was plain Virginia needed some room to breathe.

"Could I?" she whispered. "*Dare* I?"

"It would only be for a little while," Ginny said reassuringly. "For the rest of the train trip, and when we arrive in Seattle, I'll be you, and you'll be me.

"When your fiancé meets us, I can introduce you as my best friend, who's come to be my attendant at the wedding. I can say I want you to go everywhere with us. That way, you can get to know him by observing the way he treats me. There's no way he can recognize you, is there? He's never seen you either?"

"No," Virginia said. "He's never seen me, not even a picture, as far as I know." She pressed her hands against her cheeks. "This is happening too fast," she protested. "I just can't think."

"Then don't think!" Ginny said. "It's so easy. This way, you'll have a whole week to see what Nicholas is like. That's what you want isn't it? A chance to get to know what kind of man he is before you're married?"

"I did say that," Virginia admitted. "And it is what I want—only—how on earth will we ever tell him the truth?"

"We'll cross that bridge when we come to it," Ginny said serenely. "This plan might help me, too, you know. In case my brother wires ahead to have someone meet the train in Seattle, hoping to find me. I'm not going back to Spokane, Virginia," she said, her tone sobering. "No matter what happens. I'm never going back."

From opposite ends of the berth, the two young women stared at one another, their expressions equally serious. Then, slowly, Virginia's relaxed into a smile.

"All right," she said. "I'll do it."

By the time the girls retired for the night, after sharing the picnic supper that Virginia had brought along, they'd settled on a plan of action. From the moment they arose the next morning, Ginny Nolan would be Virginia Hightower, and Virginia Hightower would be Ginny Nolan. They'd even gone so far as to consider switching clothes.

But Virginia was just enough shorter than Ginny that they'd decided against it, though Ginny had given Virginia her mother's cameo ring to wear. It was distinctive and easily recognizable.

Each girl was also so accustomed to hearing her own version of her name that they feared using any other would only confuse matters. So they'd decided that Ginny would ask that Nicholas Bennett call her Ginny, and that she would introduce her best friend as Virginia.

That way neither girl would be accidentally caught answering for the other. They were taking a big enough risk as it was. There was no sense asking for any further complications.

As she finally crawled back up into her berth and pulled the curtain closed in front of her, Ginny was more tired than she could ever remember. Every single inch of her body ached, but her heart danced with elation. She'd taken the biggest risk of her life, and won. Perhaps even the storm would be gone by morning. Wasn't the weather always worse on the eastern side of the mountains?

She fell asleep, lulled by the train's gentle motion.

February 23, 1910
Early hours of the morning

Through the night, past midnight, and into the first hours of the new day, the snow kept falling. Now the wind returned in full force, driving the snow in great driving sheets across the winding tracks of the Great Northern.

The banks on either side of the tracks, already piled high from the long winter's heavy snowfall, began to slough, caving in, tumbling over. As the hours passed and the snowfall continued to increase, so did the risk of even bigger snowslides.

On the western side of the mountains, things were even worse. In an unusual twist, the storm was striking with its greatest force along the western slopes.

Still, the train kept climbing.

At about one a.m. it reached 1100 feet at Leavenworth, the last big town on the eastern side of the mountains. It took on passengers, and did a thing the railroad men called doubleheading. It coupled on an extra engine, to help it make the twisting, steep-graded climb up into the heart of the Cascade Mountains.

From Leavenworth, the train would climb another 2240 feet, until it reached 3340 feet and the railyard at Cascade, eastern portal of the recently constructed Cascade Tunnel. There, the second engine would uncouple, and the train would use electricity to drift down through the tunnel.

Once it reached the railroad yard at Wellington at the far end, the train would be at 3105 feet, making its descent into western Washington.

But even in good conditions during the winter, it was on the western side of the mountains that a train was the most likely to encounter trouble.

From Leavenworth the tracks of the Great Northern made a great hairpin turn. Even in the summer the turn was slow, but it was the safest way to help the trains lose elevation.

But even this "safe" route had a problem spot. At the mouth of the turn lay a place named Windy Point. Little more than a half mile of track, it ran along a narrow ledge that wound around the face of Windy Mountain. Every year train crews battled all winter to keep this place clear, using specially designed snowplows known as rotaries. Even using these powerful machines, Windy Point was one of the worst places for slides in all the mountains.

And, by the early hours of February 23rd, Windy Point was in big trouble.

It had been hit by an avalanche from high up the ravine above it, bringing down snow that wasn't soft and slushy. It was dense and hard-packed, and so deep it filled the snowbanks that rose on either side of the tracks from brim to brim, completely covering the tracks. Obliterating the only route to western Washington.

Even the rotary dispatched to clear it couldn't get through this slide. Instead, the big, whirling blades designed to slice quickly through soft snow jammed in the hard-pack, bringing the powerful engine to a shuddering halt. When the engineer attempted to back up to take another run, he discovered the front end was stuck fast, the front wheels clogged with snow.

The rotary would have to be dug out before it could continue working, and the crew it carried had nowhere near enough men to get the job done. Work clearing the slide came to a standstill. The rotary was well and truly stuck.

The only way through to western Washington was now blocked by a snowslide and a disabled rotary.

And still, the snow kept falling.

❧ 9 ❧

In spite of the fact that she'd been exhausted the night before, Ginny awakened early the next morning. She could feel a delicious sense of anticipation fill her as soon as her eyes popped open. By now, Spokane and the life she'd lived there were far behind. She could start a new life, one lived according to her rules. She could make of herself whatever she wanted.

She rolled over toward the green curtain which still screened her berth, and discovered she was grinning at absolutely nothing.

But she thought the decision to masquerade as Virginia had something to do with her good humor. The plan had been an inspiration, Ginny decided. Not only would it provide her with a measure of safety when she reached Seattle, it had made her take a new look at the life which lay ahead of her.

Until she'd met Virginia, Ginny had been frightened by the future, however much she'd struggled not to admit it. Getting away from Stephen had taken all her energy, her creativity, her impetuosity. She'd had none to spare for what the future might bring. All she could imagine was a life of hardship.

And it still might be like that, she admitted, as she rolled over onto her back and tucked her hands behind her head. Certainly, Ginny's future was uncertain. But she felt excited about it now. Filled with possibilities and the spirit of adventure.

She was bound by no one's rules but her own now. Not Stephen's. Not Amanda's. The future could be whatever she chose. It was up to her to shape it.

But you can't shape anything if you start your new life as a slugabed, Ginny.

Moving quietly, so that she wouldn't wake Virginia in case she was still asleep, Ginny threw back her covers, rolled onto her stomach, and slid down from the upper berth, pulling the robe she'd set at the foot of the bed down with her as she did so. As her feet hit the cold, hard floor of the train car, Ginny winced. Quickly, she shrugged into her bathrobe and stepped outside the privacy curtain.

But as she released her hold on the upper berth she realized something. The always-present swaying of the cars had stopped. The train wasn't moving. Unable to see out the window on her side of the train because the curtain was drawn, Ginny moved across the aisle to stare out the window.

The berths on this side weren't made up, as the train wasn't full. Why had the train stopped? Ginny wondered. Surely, they weren't in Seattle already, were they?

Using the sleeve of her bathrobe, Ginny wiped moisture from the window. But even with the glass wiped clean, she could see almost nothing. Staring out the window was like staring at a blank sheet of paper. All Ginny could see was white.

It wasn't until she saw one of the railroad men pass in front of her as he walked the length of the train that Ginny realized the truth.

She was staring straight out into a snowbank. The train was nowhere near Seattle. It was still high in the mountains.

Quickly, Ginny whirled and tiptoed back across the aisle. She knelt, and was attempting to ease her carpet bag out from under the lower berth when the green curtains parted. Virginia poked her head out.

"What is it?" she asked. "Are we there already?"

Ginny shook her head. "I don't know why, but we're still in the mountains. I'm going to get dressed and find out what's happening."

Virginia sat up and swung her feet over the edge of the lower berth. "I'm coming with you."

A few moments later, both girls were in the tiny women's washroom, struggling into long skirts and petticoats, pulling up stockings. The washroom wasn't really made for two. It was so tiny, the girls had trouble turning around. If they weren't careful, they bumped into one another.

Ginny was glad she'd brought skirts and shirt waists with her, rather than dresses. They showed the wear of being folded in the carpet bag somewhat less, though Ginny still felt travel-worn and rumpled. And she never would have managed the many tiny back buttons of the shirt waist without Virginia's help.

"I don't know why I think I'll be able to survive on my own," she said jokingly, as Virginia finished the last of them. "I can't even dress myself!"

"At least the corset hooks in front," Virginia commented.

Ginny made a face. She'd always hated wearing a corset. And she'd never learned to lace her stays as tightly as Amanda wanted. Amanda laced her own so tightly her figure formed an almost perfect hourglass. Ginny'd never understood how her stepsister-in-law was able to breathe. Privately, she'd always considered Amanda's tightly laced corset to be a contributing factor in her famous ill-temper.

"No, but, seriously," Ginny protested. "I never even thought about this before, but it's almost impossible for me to get into my own clothing! I don't know what I would have done if I hadn't had your help. How am I supposed to fasten up all those tiny back buttons?"

Virginia was silent for a moment. Ginny could see her friend's serious expression reflected in the washroom's tiny mirror.

"You can't. Not without a servant," Virginia finally answered quietly. "Maybe we should have exchanged clothing after all. Nicholas Bennett won't know what I look like, but he does know Papa wasn't wealthy."

Startled, Ginny stared. The similarities between the two girls were easy to see, but now that she knew what to look for, the differences were just as plain.

Ginny didn't think of her clothing as being particularly fancy, not compared to what Amanda wore, anyway. But, now that she was paying attention, she could see that Virginia's clothing was as different from hers as Ginny's was from Amanda's.

Ginny's shirt waist was made of fine, sheer white batiste. The front was adorned with lace inserts. A long row of tiny fabric covered buttons fastened up the back. Even Ginny's heavy, dark brown skirt fastened behind her.

Virginia's shirt waist was made of thicker, sturdier fabric. It buttoned up the front, as did her skirt of navy blue. Her garments were clean and well cared for, but they were also plain and functional, and she could get into each and every one of them all on her own.

They were the garments of a working woman, a woman who had few luxuries, and the luxury of a servant to help her dress certainly wasn't one of them. The two young women might look alike, but just a glance at their clothing revealed the fact that they weren't social equals.

"I'm sorry," Ginny said softly. "This is going to sound ridiculous—but I've simply never thought about such things before."

Virginia turned around to face her. "It's all right," she said. "Neither have I, really. I only hope—" She broke off, her expression clouding.

"What?" Ginny prompted.

Virginia pulled in a deep breath. "I only hope Nicholas Bennett isn't disappointed when he finds out I'm the one he's supposed to marry."

Ginny opened her mouth to make a swift dismissal of Virginia's concern, but something in the other girl's expression stopped her.

Switching identities wasn't a grand adventure to Virginia, the way it was to Ginny. Instead, it was her own act of desperation. She'd fastened upon the masquerade as her only means to discover more about her future husband. Virginia might never have agreed to the switch in the first place, if she hadn't been feeling so frightened. Glibly dismissing her fears would hardly be the act of a friend, even a brand new one.

"Do you want to call off the masquerade?" Ginny asked softly. Then she stood perfectly still as Virginia's hazel eyes searched her face.

"No," Virginia answered after a moment. "But I admit it's taking a little more getting used to than I thought it would. I'm not used to almost having a twin sister."

"If it makes you feel any better," Ginny answered, "neither am I. And I promise to do my best *not* to convince Nicholas Bennett that he's become engaged to someone who only cares about her clothes and her social calendar."

When Virginia didn't smile, Ginny made an even greater effort to alleviate the tension.

"Though that might not be a bad plan, you know," she confided. "The more idiotic I seem, the better you'll look by comparison."

At long last, Virginia's delicate features lit in a smile. "It's all right," she said. "I really *do* want to go through with this. Just don't drive him away before we can reveal the truth, that's all."

"I promise," Ginny said, pleased that she'd actually coaxed Virginia into teasing. "Now, let's get out of here before I perish of claustrophobia.

I want to find Lucius so we can discover where we are."

"And breakfast," Virginia said. "Don't forget about that."

As they made their way back through the sleeping car, both girls were smiling.

"We're at Cascade. That's the eastern side of the tunnel," Lucius Anderson, the porter, said, when the girls located him. He was at the very front of their car, assisting the woman with the young child Ginny had overheard the night before. During the time it had taken the girls to dress, the rest of the sleeping car had come to life.

"But why have we stopped?" Mrs. Starling, the woman with the child, asked Lucius, voicing the question every passenger on the train wanted to know.

"Haven't heard for sure," Lucius admitted, as he rolled up bedding, stowed it in an upper berth, then pushed the berth closed. He looped the green curtains up and out of the way. "But I'd guess there's some sort of trouble on the tracks up ahead on account of this storm. Never seen one quite like it, I have to say."

"But I want to go to Seattle," the child protested. "I want to go home."

"Hush now, William," said his mother. "We all

want to get to wherever it is we're going. I'm sure Mr. Anderson and the railroad crews are doing the best they can."

Lucius leaned down to tweak the youngster on the forelock. "I can tell you why we stopped at Cascade, though."

"Why?" young William demanded at once. His mother sighed and rolled her eyes. It was plain she considered her young son a handful. Ginny and Virginia exchanged a quick smile.

"Because there's a cook shack here," Lucius said. "Best meal stop in all of eastern Washington. You're hungry for breakfast, aren't you?"

"Yes, *sir!*" William Starling said.

"Well, what are you standing around for?" Lucius admonished. "We'd better get a move on." With one quick motion, he hoisted William Starling up onto his shoulder and started for the train car door. The second he opened it, Ginny felt the bone-chilling cold of the storm.

"It's still snowing pretty hard, I'm sorry to say," Lucius said as he looked out. "But at least the wind's died down. Some of the men have cleared a path to the cook shack. You ladies shouldn't have too much trouble. Mind your head now, youngster."

With that, he set off.

"Gracious, he wasn't joking about the snow," Mrs. Starling exclaimed as she moved to follow.

Ginny stuck her head out the door. It was snowing just as hard as it had been the day before. So hard, Ginny could see no more than a little ways in front of her. Because of the high snowbank, she couldn't see the cook shack at all. But she could still see Lucius, with William perched high upon his shoulder, and Mrs. Starling hurrying along behind. They reached a break in the snowbank, passed through it, and were lost to sight.

"Come on," she said to Virginia. "We'd better go too."

All the way to the cook house, she tried not to think about the fact that her newly dried ankle boots were being soaked once more.

The outside of the cook shack reminded Ginny of a barn, but inside, she was pleased to discover that it was warm and cozy. A dozen or so rough hewn tables flanked by equally rough benches filled the interior. Some were already occupied with other passengers from the train. All were ready for service, set with white enamelware and tin cups placed upside down.

In one corner of the cook shack, a big pot-bellied stove poured forth warmth. At the opposite side of the room from the stove was the kitchen. Ginny could see an enormous, flat-top cookstove. Pots, pans, and kettles hung from big spikes along one wall. In front of the stove stood two men, one tall and thin, the other large and round.

"Hey, there, John," Lucius called out. "Got some more customers for you."

At the sound of the porter's voice, the round man turned around. "Flapjacks or oatmeal?" he bellowed.

Ginny met Virginia's, then young William Starling's surprised and delighted eyes. "Flapjacks!" all three called back at once. Then Virginia clapped a hand over her mouth.

Their enthusiastic response provoked a ripple of laughter throughout the cook shack. John, the round man, grinned. Ginny felt her spirits, dampened by her serious conversation with Virginia, once more begin to soar. This really *was* an adventure, she thought. And she really ought to make the most of it.

"Let's go find a table," she said, linking her arm with Virginia's. "Come on."

They made their way to a table near the potbellied stove, with the Starlings trailing behind.

"Looks like we'd better get a move on, Henry," the round man said. "Don't want to keep that young fellow waiting any longer than we have to."

The man named Henry smiled, then turned back to the stove.

"You folks make yourselves comfortable," the

round man called as he turned back himself. "Breakfast'll be coming right up."

"That's John Olson, the cook," Lucius Anderson said as he swung William down from his shoulder. "His assistant there is Henry Elliker. Best cooks at any stop in Washington. You ask anyone working for the railroad."

"Lucius says that enough times, he gets an extra helping of flapjacks," John Olson sang out. A second ripple of laughter went through the passengers in the cook shack.

Lucius grinned, as if pleased to have been the cause of a joke. "You folks'll be all right now. I have to get back to the train—see who else needs help. I'll come take you back when you're finished." His laughing gaze paused on Ginny and Virginia. "Or maybe one of these young gents can give you ladies a hand." With a tip of his hat, he set off.

"Gracious," Mrs. Starling exclaimed, as she settled across the table from Ginny and Virginia. Automatically, she reached to restrain William who was squirming on the hard bench, already impatient for his breakfast.

"I don't think I can remember when I last had so much excitement," Mrs. Starling continued. All of a sudden, a frown appeared between her eyes. "Gracious," she said again. Ginny struggled to keep back a smile. "Gracious" appeared to be Mrs. Starling's favorite exclamation.

"You two girls certainly do look alike," she went on now. "I'm sorry, I know you told me who you were on the train, but with all the confusion this morning, I'm afraid it just went in one ear and out the other. I'm Mrs. Emmeline Starling."

Ginny took a breath and felt Virginia tense ever so slightly on the bench beside her. This was the moment of truth. "I'm Virginia—Miss Virginia Hightower," Ginny said. "And this is my friend, Miss Virginia Nolan."

"And the same name, too," Mrs. Starling exclaimed. Then her brow wrinkled once more. *Uh oh*, Ginny thought. *Here it comes.* The other woman had made the connection between the name Virginia and the incident last night already.

"Virginia," she murmured. "Now what does that remind me of?"

"But everybody calls me Ginny," Ginny put in swiftly, hoping to head Mrs. Starling off.

"Mama," William interrupted in a loud whisper, reaching up to tug on her arm. "Where's breakfast? I'm hungry."

"William," his mother answered, immediately sidetracked. "You mind your manners now. Sit still and behave yourself, or you'll have oatmeal instead of flapjacks."

William sat bolt upright, hands locked at his sides. He looked so serious, yet so panic stricken, it was all Ginny could do to keep from laughing aloud. Out of the corner of her eye, she saw Virginia duck her head so William wouldn't notice the way that she was smiling.

"And you say you girls aren't related?" Mrs. Starling went on, apparently heedless of the reaction she'd provoked in her son. "Not at all?"

Unable to trust herself to speak without laughing, Ginny shook her head. Mrs. Starling shook hers, too, with a *tsk* of her tongue. "Well, I never. Keeping you girls straight will be an accomplishment, I must say."

"Excuse me," a new voice said. "Miss Virginia Hightower?"

Beside her, Ginny felt Virginia jerk, as she restrained herself at the last moment from looking up. Ginny laid a hand on her friend's arm to steady her, then looked up with a smile. Standing beside their table was a young man she'd never seen before.

He wore a heavy worsted wool sweater, the rolled collar coming all the way up to his chin. He carried a jacket over one arm. Hair even darker than Ginny's own fell in a wave across his forehead, as if constantly threatening to tumble down into his eyes. Without warning, Ginny's fingers itched. What would that fine, dark hair feel like as she smoothed it back from his forehead?

Abruptly, she realized she still hadn't said a word, and that he was staring down at her, a faint frown between his eyes. They were the only colorful thing about him, a startling shade of blue, one that reminded Ginny of a cold winter sky.

The kind of piercing blue that always took her breath away when she saw it, that always made her stop and look up, taken by surprise. The kind of blue whose beauty struck straight through the heart. That was the color his eyes were. Without warning, Ginny felt her throat burn, as if she was fighting back an impulse to cry.

"I beg your pardon," the young man said at last. "I don't mean to intrude—I realize this is very forward of me—but did I hear you say that you are Miss Virginia Hightower?"

"*Ginny,*" Ginny finally answered firmly with a smile. *For heaven's sake, get a hold of yourself,* she mentally chastised. The masquerade had been her idea, yet still this young man's appearance had taken her off guard. Something she couldn't and wouldn't allow to happen again. She was Virginia Hightower.

"It's a pleasure to meet you Mister—" Ginny let her voice trail off. "Actually, I don't believe I've had the pleasure, have I?"

To her astonishment, a wave of color swept the

young man's face. "No—not exactly," he stammered. "That is—I—"

"Mama," William suddenly whispered again. "I'm about to *starve.*"

"William," said his mother. "Hush now. You mustn't be rude to Mister—I mean—you should let Mister—finish—" Her brow wrinkled. She broke off.

"Bennett," the young man blurted out, the color in his face growing even brighter. "My name is Nicholas Bennett."

ℭ 10 ℘

Ginny's breath hitched in her throat. She tried to say something, and discovered that she couldn't get a word out. Nicholas Bennett. But surely that was the name of Virginia's fiancé!

"Oh—but—" she stammered. "Seattle—I thought—"

Impossibly, Nicholas Bennett's face got even redder. "Yes, I know," he said, exactly as if Ginny had uttered a complete sentence anyone could follow. "I apologize for taking you by surprise. But when I received your telegram and realized what train you must be on, I decided to set out to meet you at once. I thought we might make at least a portion of the journey together."

"But I don't understand," Ginny protested. "Where on earth did you get on?"

"In Leavenworth," Nicholas Bennett answered.

"I could hardly seek you out then, Miss Hightower. It was the middle of the night. But I've been trying to figure out a way to make your acquaintance all morning. You must agree that we have much to—"

Abruptly, Nicholas Bennett seemed to become aware that there were others seated at the table, not just Ginny. His voice faltered, then broke off.

Ginny could feel Mrs. Starling's watery blue eyes watching her avidly from across the table. Beside her, Virginia radiated tension as strongly as the stove did heat. But, after her first, quickly cut off impulse to respond to her own name, the other girl had made no movement.

Oh dear, Ginny thought. *I've ruined things already.*

Her startled response to Nicholas Bennett was hardly the most auspicious beginning to her plan to learn more about what kind of man he was. As the silence dragged on, every single reason for calling off the masquerade right now seemed to leap straight into Ginny's mind.

Stop being such a ninny, she told herself sternly. *Virginia stood up to Stephen's fury. Surely you can deal with Mr. Nicholas Bennett.* He didn't look dangerous at all. In fact, Ginny couldn't imagine him ever losing his temper.

"Please forgive me, Mr. Bennett," she said now, with a brilliant smile. "This storm and the delay have made me quite forget my manners. Won't you sit down? Please allow me to introduce my companions. This is Mrs. Starling, and her son William."

"How do you do?" Nicholas Bennett said promptly, as if pleased to have the strange situation reduced to one where ordinary good manners could simply take over. He moved to the far side of the table and swung his leg over the bench next to William. "Perhaps, William, you would allow me to sit beside you," he said.

To Ginny's surprise, Mrs. Starling began to bluster. "Well, really, I'm afraid I just don't know," she fussed. "We've only just been introduced—a strange young man—"

"And this is—" Ginny started.

"But he's not a stranger," Virginia's voice suddenly spoke up, riding over Ginny's. "He's Miss Hightower's fiancé."

"—my good friend, Miss Virginia Nolan."

Nicholas Bennett jerked. His face, so red and flustered just a few moments before, now turned as pale as the snow outside the cook shack door. His mouth fell open.

"Oh, but, I was given to understand—" he began.

"That I had no friends?" Ginny finished softly. The warmth she'd felt a moment earlier vanished as a wave of ice swept through her.

Was this the kind of man he was? she wondered.

Did he want Virginia only because she had no friends? No one to interfere on her behalf? No one who would come to her aid if she required it?

Just as I had no one.

He didn't look the type, but then, as Ginny knew to her own cost, appearances could be deceiving. Nicholas Bennett might look like a simple, straightforward man, even a compassionate one, but he could still be as much of a deceiver as Jack Lawton.

Why had he agreed to marry a total stranger? Ginny wondered. She thought she understood at least a part of how Virginia had come to be engaged, but what were Nicholas Bennett's motives?

Nicholas shut his mouth with a snap. His piercing blue eyes aimed right at Ginny. "I am delighted to learn that Miss Hightower has a good friend with her," he said, his voice quiet. But Ginny could hear the iron in it, feel it in the way his eyes looked into hers so directly. "I had feared that she—that you— were all alone in the world."

A fine tingling radiated from the pit of Ginny's stomach. *Don't underestimate him*, she thought. Nicholas Bennett might look quiet, but Ginny's guess was he didn't miss much. Had he understood what she'd meant when she'd finished his sentence for him?

"It is a pleasure to meet you, ma'am," he continued, now, the tone of his voice softening as he turned toward Virginia. "A friend of Miss High-tower's will always be a friend of mine."

"Thank you," Ginny heard Virginia whisper.

"Gracious," Mrs. Starling said. It was her usual exclamation, but, from across the table, Ginny could see her eyes were sharp and curious. "How funny you all sound! As if you'd barely met."

"Actually," Nicholas began, before Ginny could think of a way to prevent him, "we—"

She was saved by William Starling's enthusiasm for his breakfast.

"Finally!" he shouted without warning. "Flap-jacks!"

Ginny turned her head. The cook's assistant, Henry Elliker, was heading for their table with a steaming platter of flapjacks.

"It's about time," William announced as Henry drew closer. "I'm so hungry I could eat a horse."

Henry Elliker's eyebrows shot up. "Is that so?" he said. He set the platter of flapjacks down in the center of the table, then plunked down butter and syrup beside them. "By my reckoning, there's a couple horses' worth in there, at least. That ought to hold you for a while."

"Thank *you*," William said, his eager fingers reaching for the steaming flapjacks.

Henry Elliker smiled. "You folks want anything

else, you just let us know," he said. Then he headed back in the direction of the kitchen.

"William," Mrs. Starling said sharply, catching her son's hand in mid-air at the very last minute. William's fingers wiggled helplessly in his mother's tight grip, the flapjacks just out of reach. "Mind your manners now."

"But, Mama," William protested. He squirmed, trying unsuccessfully to free himself.

"I'm sorry," Mrs. Starling apologized, her eyes taking in the three other adult occupants of the table. "He really is a good boy. It's just that he can be such a handful when my husband's not around.

"Wait your turn, William," she went on, tucking his arm back down into his lap. "Let the young ladies serve themselves first. That's what's polite. And when you reach for your own flapjacks, do it with a fork. Other folks don't want your fingers all over their food."

William's bottom lip began to quiver. He looked as if he was about to explode. Quickly, Ginny placed several steaming flapjacks onto her plate, then scooted the platter along the table to Virginia. Though how on earth Ginny was going to eat she did not know. Her appetite seemed to have deserted her right along with her wits.

If it hadn't been for Henry Elliker's timely appearance with the flapjacks, Nicholas would have told Mrs. Starling he and Miss Hightower were barely acquainted, had never even met one another until now, in fact. Information that was bound to arouse interest—and comment.

But Ginny didn't want her fellow passengers to know too many details about the situation between Nicholas and Virginia. The more interest the girls attracted, the greater the chance that someone would uncover their secret, their deception.

Pull yourself together, Ginny, she scolded herself. *Pay attention. Virginia's future happiness may be at stake. You've got to keep your wits about you.*

"How old are you, William?" she heard Nicholas ask from across the table.

"Eight years old, sir," William answered in a subdued tone.

"That's a fine age to be," Nicholas said warmly. "Just the right age to start being a help to your mother. I'm sure she must need someone to rely on, since your father isn't here."

Ginny paused, a flapjack filled fork in mid-air. Nicholas Bennett sounded so prim! So proper! Perhaps he wasn't a deceiver after all. Perhaps he was merely—

Boring!

Ginny set her fork down on her plate with a clunk, her flapjacks momentarily forgotten. The word had popped into her head as if from nowhere, but she became more convinced that it was true, the longer she thought about it. Not only that, surely it was the perfect solution. Nicholas Bennett might not be Prince Charming, but he and Virginia could still live happily ever after.

Dull men weren't dangerous. They weren't deceivers. How could they be? They lacked the initiative, the necessary impetuosity. Life with one might not be terribly interesting, it was true. But at least it would be safe and secure.

I don't need to worry about Nicholas's motivation in agreeing to marry Virginia, she realized suddenly. *He hasn't any.* He'd been content to be led, to be told what to do, probably by his own father, as Virginia had been by hers.

Ginny cast a quick glance at her friend, to see if she had come to the same conclusions. But, if she had, Virginia gave no sign. Instead, she was pouring syrup on her flapjacks as if it was the most important act she'd ever performed.

But, as she looked more closely, Ginny could see that Virginia's posture had relaxed. She still sat straight, but her spine was no longer as stiff as a board.

She's relieved, Ginny thought. *She sees it too.* Already their masquerade was bearing fruit. In fact, it was turning out even better than they could have hoped. They'd learned an important piece of information about Nicholas Bennett's character already. Perhaps the most important piece.

He might be a total stranger, but he wasn't dangerous.

Ginny glanced across the table to where Nicholas was helping William cut up his pancakes. Now more than ever that one lock of hair threatened to spill into his eyes. But with the exception of that, absolutely nothing about Nicholas Bennett looked out of place. He probably didn't have an impetuous bone in his entire body.

Not at all the sort of husband Ginny would choose for herself. *Which is a very good thing*, she told herself sternly as she lifted her fork once more. *Because he isn't going to be your husband.*

She glanced again at Virginia, to discover her friend watching Nicholas Bennett through carefully lowered lashes.

Oh, yes. She sees it too, Ginny thought. Not only that, her friend seemed very interested in Mr. Nicholas Bennett. *I have to get her alone*, Ginny thought. *To see if she agrees. There's no reason to wait until we get to Seattle. We know everything we need to know right now.*

As far as Ginny was concerned, the sooner they told Nicholas Bennett the truth, the better.

❧ 11 ❧

But all that day, it proved impossible.

The snowstorm continued without abating. The train sat at Cascade. As they returned to the train after breakfast, Ginny learned that, sometime during the night, a mail train had pulled in behind them.

This was the famed #27, Lucius told her as he greeted her upon her return to the sleeping car—the fast mail. Usually nothing stopped the mail from getting through because Mr. Hill had sworn that nothing would. He had deadlines to meet, and nothing interfered with the schedules he set, not even the weather.

But this storm had defeated even the Empire Builder. Like the passenger train ahead of it, the mail train, too, sat motionless in the railyard at Cascade, paralyzed by the storm. Not until word came that the tracks ahead were clear would the two trains be allowed to move forward.

But the hours passed, and no word came.

To Ginny's relief, the sleeping cars were sparsely populated, occupied mostly by the elderly, women, and children. Most of the men passed the time in the observation car, or "smoker," helping the car live up to its name. Every time one of them came forward to his regular seat, he seemed to bring with him the smell of tobacco.

It made Mrs. Starling wrinkle her nose in disgust, a thing she did so often Ginny began to be convinced the other woman's nose would simply stay that way.

The air of the sleeper was close and hot, the coal stove stoked constantly to keep the temperature in the car as comfortable as possible. Yet the scent of cigar smoke seemed to linger in the air, even in the cars nowhere near the smoker, clinging to the gentlemen's garments as they passed through the aisles.

"They drink alcohol back there, too, you know," Mrs. Starling had confided in a low voice to Ginny and Virginia. "*And* play cards, or so I hear. Mr. Starling never visits the smoker when we travel together. He stays right by my side."

As she spoke, she'd looked approvingly at Nicholas, who was seated next to Ginny. He hadn't left her side since their meeting at breakfast. Instead, he'd returned with Ginny and Virginia to the Winnipeg. He, himself, had a berth on the Similkameen, he'd told them, the sleeper just one car back.

Mrs. Starling had nodded her head in approval when Nicholas had informed them of the arrangement. Plainly, she thought he'd done what was proper, refusing to so much as bed down in the same sleeping car as his fiancée.

Equally plain was the fact that, while suspicious at first, Mrs. Starling had quickly been won over by Nicholas. Ginny even thought she could pinpoint the exact moment when the other woman's opinion had changed. Nicholas had won Mrs. Starling's heart in the time it had taken him to cut up her son's flapjacks.

As far as Ginny was concerned, Mrs. Starling's approval was the final seal to her own observations. If Mrs. Starling approved of him, surely Nicholas Bennett must be safe. But so far, Ginny'd been unable to accomplish her goal of determining if her observations agreed with Virginia's, and if Virginia agreed they should end their masquerade.

Ginny sighed now, tapping one foot impatiently against the train's wood floor, wishing she could come up with some subtle way of attracting Virginia's attention. Could she accidentally swing her foot too far and kick her, then apologize and insist they go to the washroom to make sure she hadn't caused an injury?

Oh, that's an excellent plan, Ginny, she told herself. *Remarkably subtle. No one would notice a thing.* Even Amanda would have seen through a tactic like that. Beside her, Ginny heard Nicholas clear his throat. He leaned forward just a little, as if about to say something.

Perhaps he'll talk to Virginia, Ginny thought, though she knew that it was she, herself, who should be making conversation.

The trouble was, she couldn't have the kind she wanted with Mrs. Starling present. If she started asking Nicholas questions about his life in Seattle, the older woman would realize that Miss Hightower and her fiancé barely knew one another. An arranged marriage might not be all that unusual, but Ginny was still reluctant to do anything which might attract added attention to herself or Virginia, and she had a sinking feeling that anything Mrs. Starling knew would soon be known all over the train.

Nicholas leaned back and Ginny sighed again, crossed her arms in front of her chest, and turned her attention to the transformed Winnipeg. During the time the passengers had spent at breakfast, the porters had been busy, once again returning the sleeping cars to their daytime configuration.

The upper berths were pushed up out of sight. Ginny knew from watching Lucius stow William Starling's berth that the bedding for each set of berths would be neatly folded up and stored inside the upper one.

In their stowed position, the berths were completely invisible, having been carefully designed to form part of the elegant decoration of the train. Their outer surfaces were covered by finely decorated, glossy wood paneling. Ginny never would have suspected their existence if she hadn't already known they were there.

The pull-out platforms that turned the seats into the lower berths had all been pushed back out of sight. The plush, high-backed seats once more simply faced one another. The green baize privacy curtains were looped up out of the way. The car looked exactly like it was set for a day excursion of a few hours.

The only problem was, they weren't going anywhere.

Ginny uncrossed her arms and crossed her ankles. The foot that rested on the floor continued its tap, tap, tap. Ginny's thoughts pounded in time to the rhythm. In the seat opposite her, Mrs. Starling finally broke the silence by beginning an anecdote about the weather.

How on earth could she get rid of Nicholas and

Mrs. Starling? Ginny wondered. All she needed was a moment. But both other people seemed attached to her like sealing wax. Nicholas by what Ginny was sure was a sense of duty, Mrs. Starling because she was curious.

It was true that the older woman had left for a few moments shortly after breakfast to wipe William's sticky fingers and face. But after giving permission for William to play with a boy his age from the other sleeping car, she'd rejoined their party almost right away.

Not before Ginny had caught a glimpse of her speaking with Lucius, however, glancing furtively back at Ginny and Virginia as she did so, a fact that had made Ginny's stomach plummet in dismay. Either Mrs. Starling was discussing the fact that there suddenly seemed to be two young women named Virginia, or she was telling Lucas that Miss Hightower and Mr. Bennett were engaged. Either way, it could spell trouble.

If other passengers learned of "her" engagement, Ginny and Virginia would lose their opportunity to quickly and easily end their masquerade. Explaining the situation to Mrs. Starling would be difficult enough—but rather her alone than the whole train.

Think, think, think, Ginny told herself in time to her foot. Mrs. Starling ended her tale about the weather and launched into one about one of

William's escapades. But, for the first time since she could remember, Ginny's brain refused to work for her. Her headstrong nature seemed frozen. Her impetuosity had failed, thwarted by Mrs. Starling's avid curiosity and Nicholas Bennett's good manners.

Ginny uncrossed her ankles and planted both feet firmly on the floor. It was time to face facts. The person who was thwarting her most soundly was the person she wanted most to help: Virginia. And for one simple reason. Virginia hadn't looked at Ginny since they'd reboarded the Winnipeg.

She couldn't take her eyes off of Nicholas Bennett.

All morning, Virginia had sat beside Mrs. Starling on the seat facing Ginny, watching Nicholas from carefully lowered eyelashes. If he'd noticed the attention he was receiving from his fiancée's friend Miss Nolan, he'd been too polite to show it. But, as the hours of the morning had dragged on, Ginny had thought she could feel a change in him as he sat beside her, like a watch slowly being wound tight enough to break the spring.

Nicholas Bennett wasn't as calm as he appeared. His wishes, too, were being thwarted by the morning. Ginny almost laughed aloud when she realized the ironic truth. The whole time she'd been hoping for a moment alone with Virginia, Nicholas had been hoping for a moment alone with her!

What had he said at their first meeting that morning? "You must agree we have much to—" *Discuss?* Had that been what he'd been about to say?

Mrs. Starling reached the climax of her story. "Can you imagine that?" she said.

Oh, yes, I can, Ginny thought, though she hadn't heard a single word Mrs. Starling said. But she could all too clearly imagine a moment alone with Nicholas Bennett.

A moment in which he'd no doubt wish to begin discussing their upcoming marriage. A moment Ginny was positive she could not let happen. Until she'd spoken with Virginia, under no circumstances could Ginny allow herself to be alone with "her" fiancé.

"Lunch time. Lunch is ready, folks," Lucius announced without warning. Ginny started, then got swiftly to her feet. Was the morning really gone already? Still, she was so grateful for the distraction she almost hugged the porter. After the tense morning on the train, even the cold walk to the cook shack seemed a welcome distraction.

By unspoken consent, passengers occupied the same tables they had for breakfast that morning. But no sooner had Ginny sat down to eat than she discovered eating was completely out of the question.

Sitting beside Nicholas had been uncomfortable

enough, but now he was once more opposite her, where his piercing blue eyes could look into hers at any moment. Ginny was sure his eyes would be full of questions. Abruptly, she discovered she couldn't eat a thing. She did her best to cover it up, arranging and rearranging the food on her plate, listening to William prattle on about his morning.

She thought she'd done a pretty good job of covering up her discomfort until Nicholas spoke. "Are you well, Ginny?" he asked during a pause in conversation. "Do you not care for the stew? Shall I ask the cook if there is something else?"

"No, thank you," Ginny replied, realizing that the truth was she felt worn out completely. Why was handling Nicholas Bennett so difficult when it ought to have been so easy? *Make up an excuse*, she commanded herself silently. *Pretend you're back with Stephen and Amanda.*

"It's my head, that's all," she said, inspired by the excuse Amanda had always used to get her way. "It aches."

At once, Nicholas rose to his feet, his own lunch forgotten. "Perhaps a moment of quiet while most of the other passengers are at lunch," he suggested. "Please, allow me to escort you back to the train."

Oh, no you don't, Ginny thought. Then was surprised to find herself suppressing a sigh as he came around the table and helped her to her feet. It was exactly the kind of suggestion she should have expected of him, she thought. Thoughtful, but uninventive.

Why not a brisk walk and a tour of the Cascade railyard? she wondered, as she felt his hand against her back, in case she was feeling faint, no doubt, and needed to be steadied. Why not a sudden headlong plunge into a snowbank? Why not a shock, an adventure, not a rest, to cure her headache?

Nicholas's head was bent over hers, his eyes searching her face. As always, that one errant lock of hair tumbled over his forehead.

Without warning Ginny realized she'd forgotten the rest of the occupants of the table, including Virginia. All she was doing was staring up at Nicholas Bennett, struggling with the impulse to do something, anything daring.

What would it take to shock him? she wondered. To stir him? To make his winter eyes kindle, then burst into summer flame? What would it take to make his body tremble against hers?

I could tell him the truth, she thought. *That ought to do it.* But then she'd lose her chance. Her chance to know what his hair felt like as she brushed it from his forehead. She felt her right arm lift, as if it had a mind of its own.

"Miss Hightower?" she heard Nicholas say softly, his tone puzzled. "Are you ill? Shall I summon aid?"

"No, of course not," Ginny said, the sound of Virginia's name acting like a bath of cold water. What on earth had she been about to do? What had she been thinking? The close air of the train car and the cook shack must be affecting her more than she realized. That must be it.

She didn't care about Nicholas Bennett. He was right for Virginia Hightower—the real Virginia Hightower—not for the real Ginny Nolan.

"I think you must be right," she said. "If I could just return to the train to lie down—but—perhaps—Miss Nolan—"

Ginny broke off, turning to look over her shoulder to where Virginia was still seated at the table. Here, finally, was the opportunity Ginny had waited all morning for: the chance for the two young women to be alone together. Now if only Virginia took the hint.

"I'll walk her back," Virginia offered. She rose, not looking at Ginny. Her face was pale, Ginny noticed, as if she was the one who'd claimed the headache. She realized suddenly that she had been standing with her back to Virginia, but Virginia had had a clear view of Nicholas's worried face.

But he isn't really worried about me, *Virginia*, she thought. *Only about the woman he thinks is his fiancée.*

"Well, if you're sure," Nicholas said.

"Of course," Ginny answered. "Virginia can get me settled, then come back to finish lunch."

Finally, Ginny thought. Her impetuosity seemed to be working once again. She and Virginia could have their chat on the way back to the train. Then Virginia could come back to Nicholas and ask for a moment alone with him. She could tell him the truth. He would be shocked, perhaps put out, but he would soon recover. After all, it wasn't as if he'd really gotten to know them well. He was probably like everyone else, practically unable to tell one girl from the other.

"Thank you. I'd appreciate that, Miss Nolan," Nicholas answered. He smiled warmly and Virginia colored. Then he stepped back, so that the two girls made a bracket on either side of him. Ginny and Virginia were just turning to go when a tiny woman in an enormous woolen shawl bustled over to them.

"Oh, good, I haven't missed you," she said, her tone breathless. "I know you'll think it terribly forward of me, seeing as how we haven't been properly introduced, but I just couldn't help myself. What a romantic story. Getting on the train in the middle of the night. I just had to come over and offer my congratulations."

No! Ginny thought. *No, no,* no.

Without warning, the woman broke off, her eyes darting between Ginny and Virginia. "Well, I never!" she exclaimed, the fringe on her shawl quivering. She sounded so exactly like Mrs. Starling that Ginny battled a wild impulse to laugh, in spite of the fact that she didn't find the situation the least bit funny.

"Gracious," the woman went on, continuing her imitation perfectly, "however do you tell them apart?"

Nicholas looked down at Ginny and Virginia, an expression in his eyes Ginny couldn't quite read. He stood so close Ginny could feel the sudden ripple that passed through his body. *What was the saying?* she wondered suddenly. As if somebody had just walked across his grave.

"Oh, but how silly of me," the tiny woman said, just as Ginny felt Nicholas pull in a breath to speak. "As if you wouldn't recognize your own fiancée. The heart always knows its choice, doesn't it? Which one is she?"

Once more, Ginny felt Nicholas's hand, warm against the small of her back. His voice was perfectly steady as he answered, "This is Miss Hightower, my fiancée. And this is her good friend, Miss Nolan. Thank you for your congratulations."

"Yes, thank you," Ginny forced herself to say. On the other side of Nicholas, Virginia stood without making a sound, her blush long since faded.

Well, Ginny thought. *That's that*. And realized

that the excuse she'd offered just a few moments before had suddenly come true. From one ear to the other, her head ached.

"We never should have done this," Virginia said. "It was a mistake."

The two girls were making their way back to the train, finally escaping from the cook shack after Ginny and Nicholas had accepted half a dozen more congratulations. It seemed that the whole train knew of their engagement, and of the romantic way Nicholas had set off to meet her.

There was no way to tell him the truth now, not when revealing it would humiliate him in front of so many people. Not to mention the disastrous effect it would have on both Ginny and Virginia's reputations.

There was no help for it. The masquerade would simply have to continue all the way to Seattle. Though how long it would be before they reached it, neither girl knew. The trains hadn't moved so much as an inch since arriving in Cascade.

Virginia marched through the snow, moving as quickly as she could through the deep drifts, her wide, forceful steps betraying her inner agitation. Ginny was glad their fellow passengers were in the cook shack or on the train. Anyone observing them would be able to tell at once that something was wrong.

"We should have told him the truth," Virginia said. Ginny brushed snow from her face, and took a firm hold on her temper. It was still snowing, but the snow was different now. The flakes were larger, wetter, sticking to everything in sight.

To help measure just how much snow was coming down, Judge McAllister, the man who had promised to speak up for the conductor if Stephen complained about him, had thrust his walking stick into the snow at the base of the snowbank. He'd gone out at regular intervals to check the snow's steady progress up the stick. An accumulation of snow as wide as his hand had fallen during the morning.

"I never should have let you talk me into this," Virginia said.

Without warning, Ginny turned her foot. She lost her balance and her temper all at the same time, leaning to one side and sitting down abruptly.

"Will you stop blaming me?" she snapped. "I didn't talk you into anything and you know it, Virginia. You agreed it was a good plan. I gave you the chance to back out first thing this morning, and you didn't take it. So stop trying to make what's happened my fault."

Virginia whirled to face her. "Don't you dare yell at me!" she shouted. "Papa used to do that. After he died, I swore I—"

She broke off, breathing hard. Through the thick, white flakes of snow, the two girls stared at one another. *So that's it*, Ginny thought. She forgot that she was sitting in the snow, her skirts getting wetter by the minute. She even forgot about Nicholas Bennett. She forgot everything but the horrified, haunted look in Virginia's eyes.

"I'm sorry," Ginny said. "I didn't know."

Virginia made a strangled sound. "Oh, Ginny," she said. "I'm so sorry. I didn't mean it." She hurried forward and helped Ginny to her feet. "You're all wet again," she added.

Ginny felt a bubble of laughter rise up and escape before she could stop it. "Actually," she said, "I'm beginning to think it's my natural condition. But being cold and wet does seem to have made my headache go away."

"Well, at least that's something."

The two girls stood, staring at one another. "We really are in a mess, aren't we?" Ginny said after a moment. "I tried to think of a way to get your attention all morning but—"

Virginia lifted her hands. "Don't tell me, I know," she broke in. "All I did was stare at Nicholas. I couldn't believe it when Lucius came to tell us it was time for lunch. The whole morning had gone by, and I'd never even noticed. You must have been so annoyed with me—I wouldn't have seen you if you'd been standing on your head."

"Don't think I didn't consider it," Ginny said. "Though I admit that was after I considered kicking you in the shins."

Virginia smiled. "And then that woman with the shawl," she said. "I thought that fringe had taken on a life of its own—and then I thought we'd never get out the door: 'Ooh Miss Hightower'" she went on, her voice rising to a sing-song, "'such a lovely story—sooo romantic!'"

"Don't!" Ginny protested, as both girls dissolved into helpless laughter. They leaned on each other, gasping for breath in the snow. As their laughter died down, Virginia's expression sobered. She reached to brush the snow from Ginny's head. On the far side of the snowbank that bordered the tracks, Ginny could hear the hiss of the steam engine, stoked to keep the power in the cars going, but other than that, the whole world seemed still.

"He's a good man, isn't he?" Virginia asked.

Ginny laid both hands on Virginia's shoulder. "Yes, he is," she said. "We'll find a way to make this all work out."

Virginia's lips lifted in a faltering smile. "Do you promise?"

"I promise," Ginny said. "Nicholas isn't like my stepbrother—or your father."

Virginia's face crumpled as if she was about to cry. "I'm sorry. But I don't think I can talk about that," she said.

Ginny hesitated, torn between the desire to honor her friend's wishes, and the desire to know the truth. "But that's why you wanted to know more about Nicholas, wasn't it?" she persevered. "To make sure he wouldn't treat you like your father did?"

Silently, Virginia nodded her head. Then she turned and began to walk back toward the train. Ginny fell into step beside her. But something in the other girl's posture caught Ginny's attention. Virginia was holding herself as stiff as a board once more. The realization struck Ginny with such force she stopped dead in her tracks.

"Oh, my God," she whispered. "He hurt you, didn't he?"

Virginia stopped also, though she kept her face averted. Ginny could see the muscles in Virginia's neck work as she swallowed convulsively, trying to answer.

"Not very often," she finally admitted. "Mostly, he just shouted, morning, noon, and night. According to Papa, everything was my fault, including the fact that my mother left us. If I'd been a good girl, she would have stayed, he said. I don't think I was ever the kind of daughter that he wanted."

"But that's ridiculous," Ginny protested. "Your mother probably left because she wanted to get away from him. It's likely he bullied her, too."

Virginia nodded. Though neither girl could bring themselves to voice the thought that hovered in the air around them: surely Virginia's mother should have taken Virginia with her when she departed. She should never have left her with a man like Virginia's father.

"Actually, I don't think he wanted a daughter at all," Virginia went on after a moment. "I'm sure he wanted a son. He told me so often enough. So when he said he'd arranged for me to marry the son of his oldest friend, all I could think of was that he was finally going to get the son he wanted."

"By choosing someone just like him," Ginny filled in, making a sudden connection.

Again, Virginia nodded. "And then he made me promise to go through with it," she choked out. Now that she'd started, the words seemed to pour out of her like water from a breached dam.

"He told me he was dying, and then he made me swear to marry Nicholas Bennett. He knew I'd never go back on a deathbed promise. But I *had* to know what Nicholas was like before I married him, Ginny. I just had to. How could I live the rest of my life with a man just like my father?"

The situation Virginia described made Ginny

shiver with a cold that had nothing to do with the snow around them. It was so close, so terrifyingly close to what had happened to her. Abner Nolan wasn't like Virginia's father, it was true. But Stephen was. Of that, Ginny had absolutely no doubt.

No wonder Virginia recognized a kindred spirit when she saw my desperation, Ginny thought. No wonder the other girl had helped her.

"What would you have done if Nicholas hadn't been different?" she asked. "If he had turned out to be a bully like my stepbrother and your father?"

Virginia shook her head, her face exhausted. "I honestly don't know," she said. "I'd like to think I'd have been as brave as you were, that I'd have run away. But I don't know if I ever would have found the courage. I've never been very adventurous, not like you."

"Well, I think you're making up for it now," Ginny said. She linked her arm through Virginia's and urged her forward. It was time to get back inside. All of a sudden, Ginny felt chilled to the bone. Though whether it was the weather or the sudden revelations about what Virginia's life had been like, she wasn't certain.

They rounded the opening in the snowbank, and started toward the Winnipeg.

"I just wish I knew how it would end," Virginia burst out suddenly.

So do I, Ginny thought. But she didn't say it aloud. Instead, she did her best to keep Virginia's flagging spirits up.

"Gracious, Miss Nolan!" she exclaimed, trying for an imitation of Mrs. Starling. "Don't you know? We're going to live happily ever after. Both of us."

Virginia's lips lifted in a smile that showed she appreciated Ginny's effort, even if she wasn't quite ready to believe it.

"If you say so," she said.

∂ο12ρ∞

"Miss Hightower, watch out!"

Snow filled Ginny's mouth, stung against her eyes, spilled down inside her coat collar. She reached to wipe it from her face, and found herself staring at half a dozen sets of enormous eyes, some already filled with frightened tears.

In an attempt to relieve the mothers on the train, as well as raise her own spirits, Ginny had taken the older children outdoors for a snowball fight during a break in the weather. But she'd been distracted by the sight of a strange train moving along one of the side tracks, shooting huge arcs of snow up into the air on both sides of it. So distracted, she'd taken a direct snowball hit to the face, launched by the boy who'd spent the morning playing with William Starling.

Ginny threw back her head and roared with laughter.

"Good hit, Thomas!" At once the children hurled themselves upon her, clinging to her skirts and laughing in relief.

"All right, that's enough for now," a voice from the break in the snowbank said. It was Claudia Hubbard, Thomas's mother. Over one arm, she carried a basket with her infant daughter, Abigail.

"You're an awfully good sport, Miss Hightower," Claudia Hubbard said, stepping through the break in the snowbank and waving the children over to her. Thomas Hubbard dashed to his mother's skirts and held on tight, claiming her for his own.

Ginny had liked Claudia Hubbard on sight. She was plainly busy keeping up with her family, but her warm brown eyes were filled with good humor. Her husband, Philip, was a great bear of a man with a shock of bright red hair and the purest green eyes Ginny had ever seen, both of which traits he'd passed on to Thomas.

"It was an awfully good hit," Ginny admitted, giving Thomas a quick wink. He ducked behind his mother's back, not certain what to make of so much grown up attention for a thing he'd been sure had been going to get him into serious trouble.

"You should come in, too," Claudia Hubbard told Ginny, as Abby began to wail from the depths of her basket. "You're as wet as they are."

Ginny grinned. "Just a few more minutes, please, Mother."

Claudia Hubbard put her hands on her hips, then slowly began to shake her head, her grin as wide as Ginny's. "You're as bad as they are, Ginny Hightower."

But she didn't press Ginny any further. Instead, she ushered the children back toward the sleeping cars with promises of dry clothes and a story. Left alone, Ginny drifted closer to the passing track. She stood, her breath hanging in the air around her, watching the strange train at work, savoring her first real moment alone, her first real taste of independence.

"It's called a rotary," said a new voice.

Ginny started, then turned to find Nicholas standing beside her. She'd been so engrossed in watching the snowplow work, she hadn't heard him approach.

A strange feeling swept her, part dread, part relief, part simple curiosity. Her impetuous decision to play with the children had accomplished the thing she'd been avoiding all day, a moment alone with him. Ginny told herself she ought to go back, but the truth was she didn't want to. It was beginning to feel too much like running.

"I never thought about how they kept the tracks clear, before," she said, turning back to watch the rotary. "That's what makes the snowbanks on either side of the tracks, isn't it?"

Out of the corner of her eye, she saw Nicholas nod. "Each time the tracks are cleared, the banks grow higher," he said. "Trouble is, when they get too high, they start to fall over. That creates a problem all its own."

Intrigued, Ginny turned to face him. "How come you know so much?"

Surprise flickered across Nicholas's face. One dark eyebrow quirked up, disappearing into that errant lock of hair. "I work for the railroad, for the Superintendent, Mr. James O'Neill. Didn't you know that?"

Ginny felt her face flush. If Virginia had known this, she'd said nothing. "No," she answered. "I didn't."

Nicholas fell silent for a moment, his eyes searching her face. "You really don't know anything about me, do you?" he asked at last.

Ginny felt her heart begin to pound at the base of her throat. She'd been afraid of what those blue eyes would see if they looked at her too closely, and now she was alone with them.

"No," she had no choice but to answer once again. But at least this time she knew it was the truth. Virginia Hightower knew almost nothing about Nicholas Bennett. Ginny Nolan wouldn't be standing in the snow with him if she had.

"I'm sure—my—father—" Ginny stumbled just a little over the words, then recovered. "I'm sure my father meant to tell me more, but he died before he could."

"But not before you gave your promise to marry me," Nicholas said.

Ginny discovered she couldn't look at him any longer. She turned back to watch the rotary. "No," she said for the third and final time. "Not before that." For a moment, the only sound was the roar of the snowplow at work.

"He was dying," Ginny said, suddenly compelled to offer some sort of explanation. "I had to do what he asked. There's nothing more sacred than a deathbed promise."

"Do you think so?" Nicholas asked. "I would have thought a deathbed promise could be a dangerous thing, a final chance for one person to bend another to his will."

"Or a final chance to right an old wrong," Ginny said. *Couldn't this be the reason Virginia's father had demanded her promise to marry Nicholas?* she wondered. *Wasn't it possible that, at the very end of his life, he'd wanted to do right by his daughter?*

"Yes," Nicholas agreed after a moment. "I suppose it could be for that."

Ginny waited until she caught the movement that told her he was gazing at the rotary once again before she spoke.

"Would you rather not marry me?" she asked.

Swiftly, Nicholas turned back toward her. "I didn't say that."

"But you don't really know me, either, do you?" Ginny prompted, gathering her courage to face him. "You promised to marry a total stranger, just as I did.

"I suppose it happens all the time," she went on when Nicholas didn't speak, "and I just never thought about it. And I can see why a woman might agree to such a plan. We have so few choices. But the whole world is open to a man. Did you not wish to choose a wife for yourself?"

Nicholas stayed silent, his eyes ranging across her face as if searching for some feature only she could possess. "Perhaps," he said at last. "But, just as you did, I made a promise."

And he would never go back on his word, Ginny realized suddenly. He wouldn't rearrange a situation to suit him, as Stephen Banks had. Nicholas Bennett was an honest man. *And what am I doing? Deceiving him.*

"I'm cold," she said. While they'd been standing outside talking, the sun had disappeared below the tops of the mountains.

"Then we should go back," Nicholas said. "I've already kept you talking much longer than I should have."

"I'm a woman, not a child, you know, Nicholas," Ginny said, irked by his assumption that it was up to him to know what was best for her and act upon it. "I can make my own decisions."

Nicholas's eyes glinted with some emotion Ginny couldn't quite identify. "I stand corrected," he said. "In that case, Miss Hightower, perhaps you would allow me to ask you a question."

Ginny raised her eyebrows, to show that she was waiting.

"Would *you* rather not be engaged to *me?*"

Ginny felt the whole world narrow to the space between them, as wide as the earth, yet no more than a single step. *Tell him*, she thought. *Do what he would do, the honorable thing. Do what's right.*

"I'm sure Miss Hightower would like very much to marry you, Mr. Bennett."

Then she took his arm, and walked the rest of the way back to the train in silence.

❦ 13 ❦

"Just one more!" Mr. Hubbard called out. "A dance for the sweethearts!"

At the far end of her sleeping car, Ginny spun around. She could feel her cheeks flush with sudden heat. Standing beside her with the baby in her arms, Claudia Hubbard laughed.

"Now, look what you've done, Philip," she chastised her husband at the other end of the car. "You've embarrassed her."

"I'm supposed to embarrass her. She's about to be a bride," Philip Hubbard retorted jovially. He put the bow of his fiddle against the strings and played a few impish notes. "Come on, now," he said. "I see how coy you've been, Miss Hightower, getting all the youngsters to dance in their elders' garments. But it's your turn now. It's no use protesting because I won't put this fiddle away until I've seen you and Mr. Bennett dance together."

"A dance! A dance for the happy couple!" a variety of voices called out. Ginny was sure she recognized the voice of Mrs. Starling chief among them. Her cheeks still bright red, her eyes sought out Nicholas where he stood beside Philip Hubbard at the other end of the car. Surely he didn't want this to happen either, did he?

Ginny hadn't spoken to Nicholas since their late afternoon conversation. To her relief, it had been easy to avoid him. Not long after the two of them had returned to the train, Nicholas had joined the rail crews digging out the wheels so that the passenger train could pull forward and allow the mail train to roll into position at the giant water tank that sat near the entrance to the tunnel.

Staring at the men from the windows of the train, Ginny thought she'd never seen such backbreaking work. Each wheel of both trains had to be freed from the snow before the trains could move so much as an inch. All afternoon, the air had been filled with the clang of shovels slicing through the snow. It had been almost dark by the time the crews had finished, and the passenger train had been run into the eastern portal of the tunnel while the mail train took on water.

Ginny had been glad when the train had once more been backed up into its original position in the railyard. She hadn't liked sitting in the tunnel.

The dark outside the windows seemed unnatural, and Mrs. Starling had shared the news that she'd overheard Lucius Anderson say that they could all be overcome by the fumes coming from the engine if they stayed inside the tunnel too long.

By the time the trains were back in their original positions, word had spread through the cars that they wouldn't be moving on that night, but instead would spend one more night at Cascade and proceed through the tunnel the next morning.

That news was discouraging enough, but the realization that accompanied it was even worse. With the coming of nightfall, the storm had returned. Once more, it was snowing.

It had actually been Virginia who'd asked Philip Hubbard to play his fiddle after supper, remarking that it was such a cheerful sound. Surely a little fiddle playing would help restore people's spirits. But it was Ginny who'd had the brainstorm of enlisting the children to play dress up.

With a collection of shawls and hats from the ladies, and hats and neckties from the men, Ginny and Virginia had adorned the children in their elders' garments, then set them dancing down the aisle. Adults and children alike had enjoyed the sight, but it didn't take long for the young people to become tired. All around her, Ginny could feel the spirits of her fellow passengers sagging, like wet

CAMERON DOKEY

clothes on the line. But she'd never expected she
might be pressed into service more directly to help
keep people's spirits up.

"Come on, Bennett," Philip Hubbard coaxed.
"Don't be shy. You have to put your arms around
her sometime. You don't want to wait until after
you're married do you?"

A burst of laughter swept the sleeping car.

"Philip," Claudia Hubbard said sternly as the
laughter died down. "That's enough now." In reply,
her husband played a series of descending notes
that made it sound as if he was crying. Again, the
passengers in the Winnipeg laughed in delight.
Standing beside her, Ginny heard Virginia laugh
along with them, the sound unnatural and high.

Ginny was just beginning to hope she was off the
hook as Philip Hubbard was doing such a fine job of
entertaining people all by himself, when Nicholas
stepped forward from his position at Hubbard's side.
He bowed, then stood up straight and extended his
hand, his eyes meeting Ginny's down the length of
the aisle.

"Would you do me the honor, Miss Hightower?"

If she could have, Claudia Hubbard would have
clapped her hands in delight. "Oh, well done,
Nicholas," she said with a smile. "You'll have to go
now, Ginny," she teased gently. "There's not a
woman alive who can turn that invitation down."

138

Well, I'm certainly alive, Ginny thought. Though she was beginning to think better of it. Wouldn't it be better if the earth simply opened and swallowed her whole?

I guess there's no help for it, she thought. But she was careful to avoid looking at Virginia as she moved forward. Slowly, Ginny walked down the aisle until she reached Nicholas, then sank into her best imitation of the curtsy Amanda reserved for her most important guests.

"Mr. Bennett," she said. "I would be honored."

A whisper of approval from the ladies swept through the Winnipeg.

"That's the spirit!" Philip Hubbard cried. He played a swift ascending scale, then launched into a dance tune, the notes running like honey, sweet and slow.

There is *no help for it*, Ginny thought. She was going to have to go through with this. She stepped forward and felt herself instantly surrounded by Nicholas's arms.

The aisle of the Winnipeg was wide enough to walk down comfortably, but just barely wide enough for two people to dance down. Within seconds, Ginny realized what dancing under these conditions really meant.

Unlike a ballroom, where their bodies would be held at a specific, sanctioned distance when they danced together, in the close confines of the train aisle Nicholas's body was pressed against Ginny's own. As they maneuvered their way slowly down the aisle, turning in the steps of the dance, it seemed to Ginny that she could feel Nicholas's every inch.

She'd never felt such a sensation before.

She could feel the strength of his arm encircling her waist, every single one of his fingers as his hand pressed against her back. She could feel his legs move against hers as he guided her in time to the music, never missing a step.

Ginny's body began to feel strange to her, light and heavy all at the same time. Her very breath seemed to grow thick inside her lungs, but her blood rushed through her veins. She was aware of herself as a woman for the very first time.

Aware of the way the swell of her breasts pressed against the hardness of Nicholas's chest. The way the steps of the dance made their bodies move in perfect rhythm, hip to hip, and thigh to thigh. Ginny felt a heat that had nothing to do with embarrassment creep through her whole body. A fine tingling danced across the surface of her skin.

I want this to go on forever, she thought. As if from a great distance, Ginny noticed that, as always, one lock of hair tumbled down across Nicholas's forehead. She lifted her hand from his shoulder to brush it back, and looked straight up into his eyes.

Ginny felt her heart squeeze inside her chest, then pick up with redoubled tempo, pounding in her ears until it became a steady roar. She'd imagined this moment earlier, she thought. But she'd never dreamed that it might come true. That she could make it come true.

There was a fire burning in Nicholas Bennett's winter-blue eyes. And she had been the one to put it there. All she'd had to do was hold him in her arms.

Dear God, she thought. *How could I have been so blind?*

She'd mistaken Nicholas's steadiness for a lack of impetuosity, of passion, but there was nothing passionless about him now. The fire in his eyes burned clear and upright. No sudden gust of circumstance would make it waver. It was like his sense of honor. Only death would snuff it out.

Never in her life had Ginny seen passion such as this. Passion that ran straight and true from a generous heart.

And she had been the one to put it there. She and she alone had lit the fire in Nicholas Bennett's eyes. In that moment, Ginny knew that all she wanted now was to watch it burn forever. To spend her life heated by its warmth, guided by its light.

"Look at that," she heard a voice beside her whisper. "Have you ever seen anything like it?"

"Never," she heard a second voice say. "I've never seen a couple so much in love."

Ginny stumbled, her body failing to move in sync with Nicholas's for the very first time. If not for the tight grip of his arms around her, she'd have fallen to her knees in the aisle. He stopped dancing at once. The fiddle music faltered.

"What is it, Ginny?" Nicholas asked, his tone urgent. "Are you all right?"

"Of course I am," she answered, stepping back with an attempt at a smile. She had to do something, anything to get out of his arms. The longer she stayed in them, the longer she feared she'd wish to stay.

It isn't possible, she thought. *I can't let it be possible.* She'd met him only that morning. How could she be in love? In love with a man who was promised to another.

Ginny took another faltering step back. She was Virginia Nolan, not Virginia Hightower. Nicholas Bennett wasn't hers, could never be hers. How could she have forgotten?

She could see Nicholas's worried eyes, searching hers for an explanation. But at the very back, the fire still burned bright. It was damped down by other concerns now, but not extinguished. It would never be extinguished, Ginny thought. Between them, they had started a fire that would burn for all time.

And she had no right to it. No right to it at all.

I've got to get out of here, she thought.

Without speaking, she pushed her way past Nicholas and moved blindly through the sleeper, past the astonished faces of her fellow passengers, past Philip Hubbard with his bow held motionless in the air.

She reached the access between the cars, fumbled her way from the Winnipeg to the empty day car ahead of it, where she'd not set foot since she'd boarded the train. To conserve the supply of coal, the day cars weren't heated, as there was room to accommodate everyone on the sleepers. The cold air was a shock to Ginny's heated skin, like a plunge into icy water.

She didn't stop until she was halfway down the day car. There, without warning, her momentum deserted her. Ginny slumped onto a seat, leaning her head against the cold glass of the window, breathing as heavily as if she'd just run the race of her life, her thoughts tumbling.

It couldn't really happen, could it? People couldn't fall in love in the space of a single day.

A scrape of sound attracted her attention. Ginny sat up straight, no longer leaning against the window, but she didn't turn around. A moment later, she could see a dark shape outlined in the window. A man's frame.

She didn't doubt for a moment that it was Nicholas, but Ginny continued to gaze straight ahead, not at him, but at her own pale features reflected in the darkened window.

Don't turn around. Don't turn around, she told herself, over and over. If she did, she knew that she'd be lost, consumed by the flame.

For the span of one heart beat, then two, Nicholas stood behind her in the cold, empty day car. Ginny clenched her hands together so tightly in her lap that they began to ache. Perhaps, if she squeezed hard enough, she could drive away the memory of what his body had felt like beneath her hands.

Tell him, she told herself once more, as she had that afternoon. *Tell him the truth. Do it now, before it's too late.* Then, from far off, Ginny heard some small corner of her heart begin to laugh in wild and desperate abandon. Because the truth was that it was already far, far too late.

She saw Nicholas raise a hand as if to touch her, then drop it back down to his side. A moment later, as silently as he'd come, he vanished. Ginny waited, knowing what would inevitably come next.

"I'm tired," she said, as Virginia materialized by her side in the day car.

"Yes," Virginia answered, her tone perfectly neutral. "I imagine that you are. I've asked Lucius to make the berths up. Everyone else is retiring for the night."

Ginny knew without asking that part of what Virginia meant was that Nicholas was no longer on the Winnipeg. He'd returned to the Similkameen, his own sleeping car.

Ginny rose, her body as stiff as if she'd labored with the railroad crews to clear the tracks. In silence, she followed Virginia back into the Winnipeg, doing her best to ignore the conversations that suddenly fell silent as she passed by. Still silent, she dressed for bed, then accepted a boost from Virginia up into the upper berth, and heard Virginia settle into her own berth below her.

"Good night, Virginia," Ginny said.

"Good night, Ginny," Virginia answered after a moment.

"Things will be different tomorrow," Ginny promised suddenly. "You'll see."

Virginia was quiet for so long, Ginny was sure she wasn't going to answer. "I hope so," she finally said quietly. She pulled the long green curtains across the front of their berths.

Long after she could hear from Virginia's breathing that the other girl had fallen asleep, Ginny lay awake, listening to her own breaths move slowly in and out, powered by the beating of her treacherous heart.

ning during the...

❧14❧

Cascade, Washington
February 24, 1910

Ginny woke to a world of whirling white, and the sinking realization that the train wouldn't be moving on that morning from Cascade. During the night, the storm had completely erased the railroad crews' hard work of the previous day. The drifts of snow were now so deep they came halfway up the sides of the trains.

Neither the mail train nor the passenger train would go anywhere until each wheel had been painstakingly dug out all over again. And still, the air was filled with blowing white.

Ginny felt depression settle over her, as heavy as her blanket. Had it really been little more than a day ago that she had fled Spokane? It seemed she could barely remember a time when her world hadn't been filled with the storm, bound by the train.

Get up, Ginny, she told herself. *Wallowing in self-*

pity never did anybody any good. The only problem with getting up was that she'd have to face both Nicholas and Virginia again.

After a night filled with restless dreams, Ginny had come to a conclusion, the only one she felt she could reach. She wasn't quite sure what had happened between her and Nicholas Bennett last night, but she was quite sure it could never be allowed to happen again. Not for so much as an instant could she allow herself to forget that Nicholas was Virginia's fiancé.

"Ginny," a whisper floated up to her. "Are you awake?"

"Yes," Ginny answered.

"I think the washroom is empty," Virginia whispered back.

"All right, I'm ready if you are," Ginny said. Once more, the two girls dressed in the tight quarters of the women's washroom, but there was little sense of camaraderie today. Silence wedged between them like a third person. Out of the corner of her eye, Ginny kept catching Virginia's eyes watching her face, then sliding away.

She saw, Ginny thought. *She knows.* And wished with all her heart she could summon up some comforting words to explain away what Virginia had seen. But she couldn't do it. She didn't understand how it had happened herself.

The only thing she knew for certain was that, no matter which direction she took, she was likely to end up on the path to betrayal.

"Well, I think it's just plain bad management," Mrs. Starling announced later that day.

She was sitting in the cook shack along with Ginny, Virginia, and Claudia Hubbard. The day had turned out to be another one of long delays. Once more, the train wheels had to be dug out before they could move forward. Nicholas and Claudia's husband, Philip, worked with the train crews. By mutual consent, the women had elected to remain in the cook shack for the day.

The big wooden building was warm, not as stuffy as the train cars were, and staying put kept the women from getting cold and wet as they trekked back and forth to the train.

The morning had passed fairly quickly, but as the afternoon had worn on, all of the women's spirits had begun to flag. Ginny's back ached from the long hours of sitting on the cook house bench. Her clothing, fresh from her carpet bag just that morning, nevertheless felt soiled and rumpled. A fine film of grime seemed to lie over everything. As the afternoon hours stretched toward evening, Ginny found herself dreaming of a long, hot bath.

Only Mrs. Starling seemed as starched and fresh

as ever, her shirt waist free from wrinkles, a jet brooch pinned to its high neck, her back ramrod straight as she sat on the hard wooden bench. Ginny was sure that, should the older woman rise to walk about the room, her petticoats would still rustle with authority. Ginny's felt limp as a well-used rag.

"William, you stay well back from there, now," Mrs. Starling called out to her son as he stood with Thomas Hubbard on the far side of the room watching Cook Olson wield an enormous knife. William Starling shifted backward one small step.

"I mean, really," Mrs. Starling continued, barely pausing to take in air. "You'd think they'd be prepared for things like this. The trains run all winter, don't they?"

"Don't think anyone's ever seen a storm quite like this so late in the season, ma'am," Henry Elliker's quiet voice said. He approached their table with four cups of steaming hot coffee.

"The crews'll be in any minute now," Elliker said simply, as he deposited the cups before them. "Word is, they've finally dug out the trains."

Mrs. Starling snorted, unimpressed. "You mean again. They did that yesterday."

"You folks should be able to get under way real soon now," Elliker went on as if he hadn't heard her. "I thought you ladies might enjoy a cup of hot coffee before you get back on the train."

"Thank you," Claudia Hubbard said at once. "That's very thoughtful of you, Mr. Elliker."

Henry Elliker's thin face lit in a tired smile. "My pleasure, ma'am." As he moved back toward the enormous cook stove, Ginny realized Elliker and Olson must be almost as tired as the railroad crews were. After all, they were just two men, yet they'd been responsible for feeding everybody for two days.

With a sudden gust of freezing air, the door to the cook shack banged open. Snow blew in through the open door.

"Trains are moving out," a voice Ginny recognized as Lucius's called out. "All passengers are kindly requested to return to the train."

"Finally," Mrs. Starling said, rising to her feet. "William, you come on now."

"I'll take the baby," Ginny offered as the rest of the women rose to their feet. Claudia Hubbard gave her a tired smile. She followed in Mrs. Starling's wake, retrieving Thomas on her way to the door. Ginny knelt and hooked the basket over one arm.

Abigail Hubbard was a tiny baby. Unlike her brother, she had her mother's dark brown hair and she'd yet to outgrow her newborn's blue-gray eyes. They stared solemnly up at Ginny from the depths of the basket.

"She's awfully small, isn't she?" Ginny murmured.

"I think Claudia is worried," Virginia answered. "She says Abby doesn't eat the way she should." They were practically the only words she'd spoken to Ginny all day. The silence between them had stretched out so long, it seemed to Ginny that it had a voice of its own, asking endless, unanswerable questions.

"We should go," Ginny said, suddenly realizing they were the only passengers remaining in the cook shack. "Thank you, Mr. Olson, Mr. Elliker," she called as she and Virginia hurried toward the door.

The two men turned from their positions near the cook stove. "Don't mention it," Cook Olson called back. "Hope you folks have an easy journey the rest of the way."

Virginia slipped a shawl from her shoulders, covering the baby's basket with it. Then she pulled the door open. Together, Ginny and Virginia went back out into the storm.

The snow was blowing wildly as they made their way from the cook shack. The wind always seemed to be worse just before nightfall. By the time they made it back to the train, Ginny was shivering, deep, hard tremors from the pit of her stomach. From the depths of her basket, Abigail Hubbard wailed. Claudia moved toward them the second Ginny and Virginia were inside the Winnipeg.

"It's all right," she said. "I'll take her."

"I'm sorry," Ginny said, feeling the need to apologize for some reason she couldn't explain. The baby wouldn't have stayed any warmer if her mother had carried her.

"It's all right," Claudia Hubbard said again. But her face puckered as she took the basket from Ginny's arm. Silently, she peeled back the shawl and looked inside. For the first time, Ginny saw fear in the other woman's eyes instead of good humor.

"She'll warm up," Claudia said, holding the shawl out. Virginia took it without speaking. "She'll be just fine."

Quickly, she moved down the Winnipeg toward the Similkameen. Ginny and Virginia returned to their seats, still not speaking. Virginia looked down at her clasped hands, turning Ginny's mother's ring around on her finger. Ginny gazed at Virginia's agitated fingers, wishing she could think of the right thing to say.

There was a sudden, neck-wrenching jerk, and the scream of metal against metal. The train seemed to lunge forward. Both girls pitched in their seats. Ginny put her arms out to brace herself, and ended up catching Virginia by the shoulders. The two girls clung to one another for an instant, then pushed back into their respective seats.

A sound Ginny hadn't heard in nearly two days suddenly filled her ears: the growling of the steam engine. Slowly, the wheels continuing to scream in protest as they moved along the track, the train inched forward.

Without warning, the growl fell silent. The train was entering the tunnel. Ginny knew the exact moment their car was swallowed up. The window at her side went from white to black as the blowing snow outside was replaced by the close stone walls.

Ginny swallowed once, then twice. She could feel her pulse begin to beat in her throat. Across the aisle, her eyes met Virginia's.

Ginny hadn't thought much about going through the tunnel. It was simply how one got from one place to another. If all had gone according to schedule, the train would have made this run in the middle of the night when the passengers were all asleep. Ginny never would have known she'd ever been through solid rock.

But all had not gone according to schedule. With every second that passed, Ginny began to feel more and more as if she were being buried alive in her own tomb. *How long?* she wondered. How long before they reached the other end of the tunnel?

All around her, Ginny could hear the creaking of the train. The light in the car flickered as the overhead lantern swayed ever so slightly. Ginny knew she should be grateful it wasn't completely dark. At least the cars had their own illumination.

But as the seconds ticked past and the journey

continued, Ginny found it difficult to be grateful for anything. Even a return to the storm would be better than this. All she wanted was to be out of the tunnel.

With a second unexpected lurch, the train came to a stop. Ginny stared out the window in horror. The world outside was still pitch-black. They were still inside the tunnel.

"What's happening?" she heard Virginia say, her voice a thin thread of panicked sound. "We're not out of the tunnel yet, are we? Why are we stopping?"

"I don't know," Ginny said. Her ears began to ring with the effort she was making to keep her composure. Her jaw ached from keeping her teeth clenched against the desire to scream.

With a flurry of skirts, Virginia moved across the space between the two seats, her hands reaching for Ginny's. The two girls clung together so tightly, Ginny was certain the bones in both their hands would be broken by the time the train was clear of the tunnel.

She heard a child, she thought it was William Starling, begin to wail. Ginny turned around to stare back down the aisle, craning her neck to see over her shoulder. "Lucius," she called. "Do you know why we're stopping?"

"Don't know for sure," Lucius called back at once. "But I reckon it's something to do with the tracks at Wellington. We'll move on just as soon as we can, I'm sure."

"Well, really," Ginny heard Mrs. Starling's voice say over the wailing of her son. Virginia's hands jerked. She gave a snort of desperate laughter. Ginny bit down hard on her lip to keep from joining her. She had a feeling if she started laughing now, she'd never stop.

"It'll be all right," she said, in unconscious imitation of Claudia Hubbard. "We'll make it through this, Virginia."

Virginia's hazel eyes looked steadily into hers. Her lips wavered upward in a tentative smile. As she had yesterday afternoon she said, "You promise?"

On impulse, Ginny wrapped her arms around her, holding her close. She could feel Virginia's heart beating hard and fast, knew her own heart beat with the same explosiveness. She knew what Virginia was asking, and what her answer had to be.

"Yes," she whispered fiercely as she stared into the darkness pressing down around the train. Pressing down against her heart. Maybe if she said it with enough conviction, she could find the way to make her vow come true.

"I promise."

❦ 15 ❧

For more than an hour, the train sat in the tunnel while the crews at Wellington battled the snow, driven into wild, erratic drifts by the fiercely blowing wind.

A rotary struggled to keep the tracks clear. Crews armed with shovels dug out the switches which would enable the trains to travel on the correct tracks. Finally, shortly after nine o'clock in the evening, the train was given the go-ahead to move on.

The passenger train rolled slowly from the tunnel and onto the first of several passing tracks that sat to one side of the main track between the western portal of the tunnel and the train depot. About an hour and a half later, the mail train joined it, moving onto a second passing track.

Passengers and crews alike were cheered by the

accomplishment. They weren't clear of the mountains yet, and the storm showed no sign of abating, but at least they'd done something. At least they'd moved on from Cascade.

All but deserted during the summer months, during the winter the railroad yard at Wellington positively bustled with activity. It was located high on the side of a steep, V-shaped ravine. The depot sat on the flat, beside the tracks. Housing for the various crews was perched precariously on the hillside just above it.

Farther back, above the passing tracks, one vast snowfield stretched to the northeast summit of Windy Mountain, an increase in elevation of 2,000 feet. The black tops of burned out trees protruded from the snow like burnt out matches. To help decrease the danger of fire from sparks which might fly from the trains in the summer, the whole hillside had been burned away.

Below the tracks, just beyond where the mail train rested, a second steep embankment plunged straight down to frozen Tye Creek. In between these two precipitous slopes, on a ledge not more than fifty feet wide, sat the two trains.

During the night, while the passengers slept, the train crews continued working. For them, as for the passengers, it had been a day of frustrating delays.

The rotary trying to keep the tracks clear between Wellington and Windy Point had rammed a stump and been thrown off center. Work could not continue until it could be replaced. But all the other rotaries were busy, working to clear the tracks at Cascade. Not until the trains were safely on the western side of the tunnel at Wellington and the rotaries had been refueled could the work on the westbound tracks once more commence.

It was midnight by the time the rotary finally headed out—a doubleheader under the direct supervision of Superintendent O'Neill. It left the Wellington yard, making its way slowly westward. Many snowbanks were sloughing over, and those that weren't seemed to tilt precariously, but they held for now, and the rotary didn't encounter anything it couldn't handle.

Until, at long last, it reached Windy Point, where crews had spent eighteen solid hours clearing the last slide away. There, the rotary came to a halt before a slide that once more filled the snowbanks from brim to brim, once more blocking the way west to Seattle.

The rotary nosed in, and started working. This slide proved different from the other. The snow was soft, the going relatively easy. But by dawn on February twenty-fifth, only one-third of the snowslide had been cleared away.

And still, the snow kept falling.

∂16∂

The railyard at Wellington
February 25, 1910

The next morning, Ginny was stiff and groggy. Though she'd gone to sleep with high hopes, all she had to do was to open her eyes to have them dashed. The snow swirled outside the train window without let up. Ginny began to feel as if she'd been traveling inside the storm forever.

Had there really ever been a time when she'd known a sound besides the scream of the wind? A bed bigger than the upper berth? A world larger than the Winnipeg? How much longer would it be before she could move and speak freely?

How long would it be before she faced Nicholas again?

At the thought of Nicholas, Ginny's fingers, busy buttoning up Virginia's shirt waist, faltered. One look at Virginia's pale, pinched face after waking had convinced Ginny that her friend was in even worse spirits than she was. To cheer her up, she'd loaned her the nicest of her remaining shirt waists. The fine, white lawn was embroidered all over in an eyelet pattern. The collar and cuffs were bordered in lace. So far, neither girl had mentioned Nicholas.

"Ginny?" Virginia asked now. Her eyes met Ginny's in the washroom's tiny mirror. "Is something wrong? Did you change your mind?"

"Change my mind?" Ginny repeated, stupidly. *Oh, yes,* she thought. *I've changed my mind. I wish we'd never embarked upon this masquerade in the first place.*

"About the shirt waist," Virginia said. "I'd understand if you didn't want me to wear it. It is awfully fine."

"Heavens, no," Ginny said, as she resumed her careful buttoning. "My mind just got away from me for a moment, that's all."

"Maybe you have mine too," Virginia ventured with a smile. "I swear my head hurts so badly I can't see or think straight."

"It's the strain of not knowing, I daresay," Ginny said. She finished the buttons and gave Virginia's back a quick pat. "There you go. Let's go find Lucius. Perhaps he'll have some good news for us."

But when they found him at the far end of the car once more helping with William Starling, the porter had none. Instead, he told them a rotary had been out all night, clearing a slide at a place called Windy Point.

"Came back for more coal, went right back out again," Lucius said soberly, his usual cheerful expression strained. "Though I did hear the engineer say the snow was soft. That'll make it easier to clear, even if it is a big one."

"I'm hungry," William Starling whined. "I want my breakfast in here. I don't want to go back out in the storm. I'm tired of being cold."

Ginny mastered a spurt of irritation, though she had to admit that William's pronouncements and her own thoughts were a pretty close match. She, too, was tired of tramping back and forth, getting cold and wet for every mouthful. She, too, was tired of feeling trapped inside either a cook shack or a train car. But, unlike the eight year old, she could see there wasn't any choice.

"You'll like Wellington," Lucius assured the youngster, his glance taking in his mother. "There's a real hotel here."

"A hotel!" Mrs. Starling exclaimed. "I shall book a room at once. Bring my things along, please, Lucius."

If Lucius resented her high-handed manner of dealing with him, he didn't show it. "I'm sorry, ma'am," he answered quietly, as if knowing he was about to be the deliverer of unwelcome news. "But I'm afraid it won't be possible to secure a room. The hotel is full up with railroad crews, particularly now that there are extra men to help clear the slides. But the hotel does have a real dining room."

Mrs. Starling sniffed to show her disapproval. "Well, I suppose that's something. How do we get there?"

"Just go straight along the main track," Lucius said. "Bailets' Hotel is right behind the depot. There's no way you can miss it. Not even in all this weather."

Ginny didn't think Stephen or Amanda would be impressed with the inside of Bailets' Hotel, but it was warm and cheerful and, if nothing else, a change from the cook shack at Cascade. The tables were set with blue and red checked table cloths and boasted not hard benches, but individual chairs. The windows even had lace curtains draped across them.

"Well," Mrs. Starling said, as the party paused inside the doorway to shake and stamp the snow off. "This is better, I must say."

At that moment, Claudia Hubbard appeared from what Ginny assumed was the kitchen, a huge, white apron wrapped around her dress, her arms full of a steaming platter of ham and eggs.

"What on earth?" Ginny said.

Claudia laughed as she deposited the serving plate on a table occupied by Philip and Nicholas. The Hubbards' young son, Thomas, was perched on his father's knee. The baby's basket rested on a chair beside him.

"With all the extra people from two trains, Mrs. Bailets is swamped," Claudia explained, as she motioned Ginny and Virginia over. "So some of us are pitching in to help."

"You go ahead and sit down," Ginny said at once, quickly maneuvering Virginia into the only remaining chair at the table. "I'll go with Claudia and see if Mrs. Bailets needs more help."

Virginia's pale face flamed with color. "I should come with you," she protested.

"You aren't feeling well," Ginny said firmly. She pulled in a breath, and switched her attention to Nicholas. She hadn't seen him at all the day before, except from a distance. And she hadn't spoken with him since the night they'd danced together.

"Good morning," Ginny said, her eyes taking in his pale face, the dark rings of weariness beneath his eyes. Even the lock of hair that tumbled down over his forehead seemed to droop. Ginny's fingers itched with the desire to smooth the lock of hair back, and his worries with it.

Nicholas's blue eyes flashed up to her face. "Good morning," he answered steadily.

"Miss Nolan isn't feeling very well," Ginny hurried on. "May I leave her in your care for breakfast?"

"Of course," Nicholas said at once. His eyes left

her face to rest upon Virginia. "I'm sorry to hear you aren't well, Miss Nolan. Perhaps some of Mrs. Bailets' fine breakfast—"

"Under the weather are you?" Philip Hubbard put in.

"Oh, Phil," his wife protested. "For heaven's sake!"

"Well, it worked didn't it?" her husband answered, reaching back to capture her hand. "I got her to smile."

At this, Virginia actually chuckled. Philip Hubbard beamed across the table at her. "There, you see?" he asked his wife.

How easy they are together, Ginny thought as she watched Claudia Hubbard's fingers tangle with her husband's. *How right.* Could she and Nicholas ever grow to be like that, she wondered, if they had enough time?

She heard a sniff behind her and realized Mrs. Starling was still standing nearby. No doubt she was miffed that Ginny had insisted Virginia take the only seat at the table. Swiftly, Ginny made eye contact with Claudia Hubbard. Claudia freed her hand from her husband's.

"I hope you won't think it forward of me," she said, moving to take Mrs. Starling by the arm, "but I've been keeping my eye on a table for you all morning. It's right over there—next to that small round table with that green plant. Don't you think that's the loveliest touch? Though how Mrs. Bailets keeps anything growing with so much to do, I'm sure I can't imagine."

"Some women are just naturally handy that way," Mrs. Starling answered. "Mr. Starling always says no one can match me for African violets."

"I'm sure he must be right," Claudia said. Mrs. Starling sniffed again, but she sat at the table Claudia suggested. Ginny gave a sigh of relief. Now, perhaps, Virginia could have some time with Nicholas. Ginny tried to ignore the swift twist of her heart. *I'm doing the right thing.*

"No more dawdling," Claudia Hubbard said, tucking her arm through Ginny's and leading her off to the kitchen. "I'm going to put you to work."

The rest of the morning passed in a blur as Ginny helped serve breakfast. Mrs. Bailets was a small, thin woman who nevertheless managed to accomplish what seemed to Ginny a truly astonishing amount of work. During the course of the morning, she learned that the tiny woman cured her own ham and bacon, canned fruits and vegetables, and baked her own bread.

She also clerked at the Wellington store and post office, made beds in the hotel and did all the hotel laundry by hand. Yet she claimed the only reason she needed help now was the sudden, unexpected influx of extra people. Even when the winter weather was at its worst, for two trains to be stuck at Wellington at once was simply unheard of.

"Well, I can't imagine how you do it all," Ginny said, during a lull in the action. Several women, including Mrs. Bailets, stood at the entrance to the dining room, surveying the contented eaters filling the room.

"It's all a matter of what you're used to, I guess," Mrs. Bailets said. Ginny saw her eyes move to the table where Nicholas still sat with Virginia, Abigail's basket beside them. Philip Hubbard had long since risen to attend to his active young son.

"I still can't get over the fact that you're not sisters," Mrs. Bailets went on, her eyes resting on Virginia. "You girls sure do look alike. And you say that's your fiancé? You're not worried about him spending so much time with your friend, now are you?" she teased gently.

Claudia Hubbard joined them with a laugh. "You'd never ask that question if you could see the way he looks at Ginny."

"Claudia," Ginny protested.

"Well, it's true and you know it," Claudia Hubbard said. "And you're just as bad."

Ginny shut her mouth with a snap. Were her newly discovered feelings for Nicholas so plain that even Claudia could read them?

"Well now," Mrs. Bailets said, her eyes switching to Ginny's rapidly flushing face. "That's different then."

Without warning, a figure appeared in the dining room doorway. With a start, Ginny recognized the conductor from the passenger train. She remembered him as calm and self-assured. But this man had none of the assurance that had helped him face down Stephen.

Now, he looked wild and storm-blown. Though the entrance to the dining room was some distance from the front door of the hotel, he hadn't stopped to brush off the snow that had collected on his garments.

He paused just inside the doorway, his eyes sweeping the room once, twice. Then they focused on the object of his search like a homing beacon and he headed straight for Nicholas.

As Ginny watched, the conductor leaned over, whispering urgently. Nicholas stood so abruptly his chair tipped over backward. He didn't stoop to pick it up, nor did he turn to make his excuses to Virginia. He simply seized the conductor by the arm and walked him back across the room, speaking swiftly and quietly.

When they reached the doorway he leaned down, studying the other man's face, plainly asking a question. When the conductor nodded, Nicholas clapped him on the back. The conductor looked over his shoulder just once, then hurried through the doorway.

Nicholas stood for a moment, his back toward the room, staring forward as if at nothing. Behind him, the dining room grew so silent Ginny swore she heard the blood rushing through her veins. Then, out of the corner of her eye, she saw Philip Hubbard move forward.

"For God's sake, Bennett," Philip said. "What is it, man? What's happened?" At the sound of another voice, Nicholas started and turned around slowly. At the sight of his face, Ginny took an involuntary step forward, her breath crowding into her throat.

She had thought him pale before but, compared to what he looked like now, his earlier pallor was nothing. Ginny had never seen anyone look like this. Nicholas's face was completely white, the color of bleached bone.

His vivid blue eyes seemed to blaze from his face, filled with some unidentifiable, desperate emotion. The expression in them was so bright, Ginny almost raised a hand to shield her own.

Nicholas's eyes swept the room, once, twice, as had the conductor's before him. As if he was searching for the one person in the world he couldn't live without. The person he would cling to with his dying strength, ask for with his dying breath. His lifeline.

The realization struck her hard and fast, a fist straight to Ginny's stomach. She was the one he searched for with those wild, blue eyes.

"Nicholas?" she said.

Instantly, Nicholas's head swiveled toward her. His eyes locked onto hers. Ginny made a strangled sound, part joy, part relief, part despair. Now, there was no help for it. She could never go back now, regardless of what the future might bring, regardless of what it cost her.

Deep within his eyes, behind the devastation, the fire that they'd started blazed like a bonfire.

Ginny forgot about Claudia Hubbard and Mrs. Bailets. She forgot about Virginia just across the room. The only person she could see was Nicholas Bennett. On unsteady legs, she walked across the room.

"What is it?" she asked. "What's happened?"

Nicholas didn't answer until she reached him, until he'd captured one of her hands in his. He squeezed so tightly Ginny all but heard the bones crack. Then he pulled her to his side, wrapping one arm around her waist as he faced the occupants of the trains. She felt him pull in one breath, then another before he spoke.

"There's been an avalanche at the railyard at Cascade."

❧ 17 ❧

It had taken everything.

Fifty feet wide, the avalanche had swept down from above the yard and hurled itself across the tracks, sweeping everything in front of it down over the side of the ravine.

The cook shack was gone. Cook Olson and Henry Elliker were gone, crushed by the force of the moving snow and buried under who knew how many feet of ice and debris. If the trains had not moved on from Cascade the night before, would they have joined them? Ginny wondered.

It could have been us, she thought as she stood at Nicholas's side, staring at the faces of her fellow passengers. *It could have been me*.

Total silence followed Nicholas's announcement, as if fear and shock had rendered people speechless. But it didn't take long for the storm to break.

"How do we know we'll be safe here?" the man sitting closest to them demanded as he leaped to his feet. "Have you looked at the slope above the trains? That whole side of the mountain could slide down and send us right into Tye Creek."

Ginny stretched one arm across Nicholas's back in a silent show of support. But, as the questions continued hard and fast, the hand that she'd pressed against his jacket slowly clenched into a fist. She could feel the tension, radiating from his body. But he kept his voice calm and steady. Never had Ginny been so impressed by a show of strength.

Wrong, all wrong, she thought. She'd never misjudged anyone as badly as she'd misjudged Nicholas Bennett. The still waters in him ran so deep Ginny didn't think she'd ever find the bottom.

"All I can tell you is that there's never been a slide here before," she listened to him say patiently. "I know that slope above the trains looks bad, but it's really safer than the set-up at Cascade."

"Why's that?" the first man to challenge Nicholas barked.

Nicholas took a deep breath. Ginny moved closer, instinctively offering him even more support. He didn't glance at her, but the hand around her waist moved upward. Just once, almost absently, as if he didn't even realize what he was doing, Nicholas stroked her hair. Then his hand resumed its tight clasp about her waist.

"The Cascade yard was in a ravine, a place where a slide is more likely to occur naturally," he explained. "It's an entirely different kind of terrain than where the trains are here. Not only that, there's a ridge, a hogback, high up on that hill. If a slide did start to come down, the hogback would shunt the snow the other way. Chances are, it wouldn't touch the trains at all."

"But you don't know that for certain," a woman's voice said. Ginny turned her head in the speaker's direction. It was Mrs. Starling. The older woman was white, all the way to her lips. William was squirming uncomfortably in the tight grip of his mother's hand.

Nicholas passed his free hand across his face. "No, I don't know that for certain," he said, his voice beginning to show the strain. "I'm not going to lie to you folks," he went on, his voice rising just a little. "Nobody can know anything for certain in this situation. Nobody's ever seen a storm like this so late in the season, not even the most seasoned men."

A low buzzing of conversation filled the dining room, reminding Ginny of a swarm of angry bees.

"Why can't we just go back to Leavenworth?" an older woman asked.

"Because the eastbound tracks are completely buried by the slide at Cascade, ma'am," Nicholas said. "There's a rotary trying to clear it now."

"In other words," a voice Ginny couldn't identify

shouted, "we're stuck here. We can't go forward or back!"

An agitated groundswell of noise rose in the dining room.

"Please," Nicholas said. He released his hold on Ginny to ask for silence by raising both hands. "Please, ladies and gentlemen, you must stay calm. There's never been a slide here before, and there's no reason to think there'll be one now," Nicholas said.

"I promise you the crews are doing the best they can. Superintendent O'Neill himself is out with a rotary right now, trying to get the slide to the west of us cleared. Once that's done, we'll get under way to Seattle just as soon as we can. All you folks have to do is be patient and sit tight. Now, if you'll excuse me, I'd better get back to work."

He turned swiftly and left the dining room. Ginny followed him, close at his heels. He strode across the hotel lobby at a brisk pace, then stopped in front of the door so suddenly Ginny couldn't stop in time. She ran right into him.

Nicholas turned, his arms reaching to steady her. "Ginny," he said, his voice so strained she almost didn't recognize it. "I'm sorry—I—"

"Don't," Ginny said. "Don't apologize, Nicholas. I should have let you go, I just—" He gave her a tiny shake, cutting off her flow of words.

"No you shouldn't have," he answered softly. "But I—"

He released her to pass one hand across his face as if trying to clear his thoughts. As he focused on her again, Ginny saw the ghost of a smile had appeared in his eyes. "I can't believe this—but I forgot that you were there. All I could think of was getting back to the trains."

Ginny felt her lips quiver upward. How could she smile in the midst of so much pain? But, somehow, it just felt right. The relief in Nicholas's face when he saw her reaction was so plain, Ginny wished she'd thrown back her head and laughed aloud. He was strong, but that didn't mean he didn't need reassurance. Didn't mean he didn't need her.

"Just be careful out there, will you?" she said. "You've already been working so hard."

"Not as hard as some," he answered, the smile vanishing like the sun behind a cloud. "Most of the rotary crews haven't slept at all."

"All the more reason for you to stay fresh," Ginny answered firmly. "They'll need someone to help decide what to do, with Superintendent O'Neill gone."

Nicholas regarded her in silence. "You're pretty fierce, aren't you, Miss Hightower?"

"Not always," Ginny said, striving to keep her tone light. "Only when it comes to those I—"

Her voice strangled in her throat. Ginny faltered and broke off. Her heartbeat hammered, posing the same question, over and over. *What have I done? What have I done?*

Almost, she had told him.

Ginny stood absolutely still, listening to the word she hadn't spoken tremble in the air around them. Watching the way the fire blazed in Nicholas's eyes like a signal beacon. He bent his head, that one lock of hair tumbling as always across his forehead. Ginny reached to brush it back.

Nicholas's hair felt like silk beneath her fingers, exactly right: soft, yet strong. At the touch of her fingers against his forehead, he started, as if stung. But the fire in his eyes burned so hot and bright, Ginny was certain she'd be blinded by it. The rest of the world would be seared away until the two of them were all that was left, all that she could see. All that she wanted.

"Only with those you what?" she heard him murmur. Ginny felt a sharp pain shoot through her chest as her heart cracked open. Everything but the need to tell him what was hidden there burned and blew away as ashes on the winter wind.

"Only with those I love."

She closed her eyes then, the blaze of his eyes became so bright, and felt his mouth close over hers.

How was it possible?

Ginny had never imagined that anything could be hotter than what she'd seen within his eyes, but the touch of Nicholas's lips was an inferno. Ginny's blood raced like wildfire through her body, roared like a bonfire in her head.

She could feel heat sweep along the surface of her skin, then slowly sink down and down, till her heart was knit back together. From this moment forward, it would be fused with his forever, the part of her that burned most fiercely of all.

Nicholas lifted his head, his blue eyes staring down into hers, his breath unsteady. "My God," he whispered. "Ginny—I—"

Ginny laid her trembling fingers against his mouth. "You have to see to the trains," she said, never certain how she found her voice. "It's all right. I know. Just promise me that you'll be careful," she said again.

"I will," Nicholas promised. "Stay inside. Stay warm. Help Mrs. Bailets if you can. It will do you good to keep busy. Try not to worry, Ginny. It will be all right. I promise."

Ginny felt a cold fist close around her burning heart. Before she could say another word, Nicholas turned and opened the door, passed through it swiftly, and slammed it shut behind him.

I made a promise, too, Ginny thought as she turned away. A promise to Virginia that things would be all right. A promise she was very much afraid that she'd just broken. She took two steps across the lobby, then stopped short.

Virginia was standing behind her in the dining room doorway.

ⳍ18ⳍ

Ginny spent the rest of the day in a strange blur, her body moving, her mind unfocused. Virginia disappeared shortly after breakfast. Ginny stayed at the hotel. Along with several of the other women, she helped Mrs. Bailets prepare and serve lunch, then dinner. Ginny lost track of the number of plates she carried to and fro, first full, then empty. By the time the last of the dinner dishes were finally done, Ginny'd washed so many her hands were red and puckered.

Nicholas had come in just once, in the late afternoon, with word that Superintendent O'Neill had returned with the westbound double rotary. The slide at Windy Point still hadn't been cleared, but O'Neill was hopeful that, with a new load of coal and water, the rotary would be able to finish the task during the night, enabling the trains to move on in the morning.

He was going back out as soon as the rotary had been refueled, to stay with it until the slide was cleared. He'd assigned to Nicholas the task of telling the anxious passengers they'd be spending one more night at Wellington.

To herself alone, Ginny had admitted she was glad she didn't have to be on the train when Nicholas made his announcement. Before the slide at Cascade, the passengers had been irritated by the delay the snowstorm caused, but no one had been particularly alarmed by it. But what had happened in the night at Cascade had changed everything, changed everyone.

Now Ginny's fellow passengers ate their meals in total silence, or in tight groups leaning toward one another, talking in low, urgent voices. More than once, Ginny saw a man bang his fist upon the table as he made a point in an argument. Anger, tension, fear all hung like smoke in the air around her.

How long will it take? she wondered. How long before the nerve of the passengers shattered like the film of ice on a pitcher of water on a winter's morning?

But surely, she consoled herself, long before such a thing could occur the slides would be cleared and they would all be on their way to Seattle.

In the blur of activity, Ginny didn't see Virginia all day, though Mrs. Bailets said she'd come in at both mealtimes to fetch food for herself and the Hubbard family. When Philip Hubbard came in to dinner, one of the last men to do so, he confirmed that Abby was ailing, and that Virginia had spent the day helping Claudia with her and Thomas.

Philip Hubbard looked even worse than Nicholas did. His hands were red and chapped from the cold; his face was drawn and haggard. He still insisted on helping Nicholas work with the train crews, in spite of his concerns about his family.

"I shouldn't have let Claudia make this trip," he said, when Ginny took a moment to sit beside him. "Abby's birth was hard on her, and the baby's always been frail. But she didn't want us to be apart, and I couldn't bear to leave her."

Ginny reached to cover one of his hands with hers. It felt strange to see such a big man so helpless. "I'm sure you did the right thing," she said, knowing how inadequate the words were even as she spoke them. "Things have to get better soon, don't they? I mean, they can't get much worse."

Philip Hubbard snorted, then rubbed a hand across his tired face. "I wouldn't be too sure about that, if I were you," he said. "This is the very devil of a storm." Then he colored. "Nicholas would skin me alive if he knew I'd told you a thing like that."

"Don't worry about Nicholas," Ginny reassured him with a smile. "I'm not the sort of female who needs things sugar coated. I'm sure Nicholas knows I'd rather know the truth."

"I daresay he does," Philip Hubbard answered with a tired smile. He stared down at the red-checked table cloth a moment. "If you'll allow me to say so, you've each made a fine choice. I wish you every happiness, Miss Hightower."

Ginny swallowed past an enormous lump in her throat. "Thank you, Mr. Hubbard."

"Philip," he corrected. "We shouldn't stand on ceremony after all that's happened, and all the help you've given Claudia."

"Thank you, Philip," Ginny said.

But in the back of her mind a voice was shouting, insisting Nicholas deserved the truth as much as she did, as much as Philip Hubbard. How could she accept Nicholas's love, Philip's heartfelt good wishes? She'd lied to them both. She was not Virginia Hightower.

All through the long, strange day, it had been Ginny's feelings for Nicholas that had sustained her, kept her going. Her greatest joy, and her greatest conflict.

When she tried to think ahead to the future, she discovered that she couldn't do it. She could see only now, the current moment. The way ahead was blurred and white, as if Ginny was trying to see through the snowstorm.

But as the day dragged on and she could still feel the heat of Nicholas's lips against her own, her heart began to dream a thing her mind knew was impossible: that somehow, she and Nicholas could be together when their strange journey was over. That, like a fairytale, their story could end in happily ever after.

"I'll walk you back, if you like," Philip Hubbard offered, as he finished his dinner. "It's dark out. You shouldn't go alone."

"Just let me get this plate washed up," Ginny said.

"Never mind that," Mrs. Bailets said, materializing behind her. "You've put in a long enough day, Miss Hightower. I appreciate your help, but you should go along now. Besides," she added, a twinkle in her eye, "there's always tomorrow, don't forget."

Ginny groaned. Mrs. Bailets chuckled. Ginny followed a silent Philip Hubbard to the hotel door. Then, sheltered by his bulk, she stepped back out into the storm.

The night passed. February twenty-fifth slid silently into the twenty-sixth, and still the storm went on.

But, finally, in the early hours of the morning, the westbound rotary cleared the slide at Windy Point. Anxious to discover how far the tracks were clear, Superintendent James O'Neill made the decision to try for the next place along the route, a stop called Alvin. Before it could do that, however, the rotary needed to refuel. In the pre-dawn darkness, it returned once more to Wellington.

With luck, by the time the passengers were up, the rotary would have gone back out, then returned with the news that the tracks ahead and to the west were clear and they could finally get under way again on this, the beginning of their fourth day in the mountains.

By noon, the rotary was indeed back, but with the grim news that there was a third slide at Windy Point. The rotary hadn't been able to get as far as Alvin.

The good news, however, was that this slide was smaller. O'Neill assured his anxious charges that his crews should be able to buck through the new slide with no problem. The rotary took on water and headed out once more.

Once more, the snow was falling.

For more than a hundred hours, the storm had raged, dumping foot after foot of snow upon the Cascade mountains. Without a significant let up in snowfall, the railroad crews didn't stand a chance and, slowly but surely, they were coming to realize it.

Every inch that fell meant that much more to clear, the same battle, endlessly. With every day that passed, every trip the rotary made, the railroad crews were running out of coal, the most valuable ammunition they had with which to fight.

By late afternoon on the twenty-sixth, the head end of the rotary, the end bucking the Windy Point slide, was nearly out of coal once more. O'Neill made the decision to return to Wellington and refuel for the second time that day.

But the rotary and its crew hadn't gone far before they discovered another slide blocking the tracks behind them. Eight hundred feet long, thirty-five feet deep, this new slide lay between the rotary and the coal it needed to keep on running.

The only consolation was that the east-end rotary, the end facing the new slide, had more coal than the end facing the opposite direction. The only choice was to try to plow on through. The only hope, that the snow would be soft and the going easy.

But by the afternoon of February twenty-sixth, hope was in as short supply as coal in the Cascade mountains.

The slide was dense, hard-packed, filled with tree trunks and boulders. There was no way the rotary could get through this. O'Neill was out of options.

He couldn't get through the slide to the east and return to refuel at Wellington. He didn't have enough coal to continue bucking the western slide and thereby get through to Alvin. He was stuck, as surely as the passenger train was. Not only that, with the double rotary trapped, all the snowplows at O'Neill's disposal were now out of range or out of commission entirely.

One had been damaged in the earlier rubble-filled slide at Windy Point. The other was struggling with the slide at Cascade, somewhere on the eastern side of the tunnel. There were simply no more tools with which to fight.

And still, the snow kept falling.

Finally, O'Neill did the only thing he could. He ordered the rotary to the safest spot he could find between the two slides, left a skeleton crew of men to keep the steam up, then took the others and began the cold walk back to Wellington. His best choice now was to telegraph for help, and pray that a fresh rotary could get through from Alvin.

But it was in the depot office that the final piece of bad news awaited him. Sometime during the day, the telegraph had gone dead. The lines were down. Now there was no way to get word in or out. No way to pass along the word that they couldn't fight the snowslides.

The passenger train with its load of sixty people plus its crew, the mail train, all the shovelers and the rest of the railroad crews—all were stranded at Wellington. The only thing that could save them now was a break in the weather.

But, as night fell on February twenty-sixth, the snow kept right on falling.

❧ 19 ❧

The railyard at Wellington
February 27, 1910

"This situation is unacceptable, sir! I demand that you move the trains at once!"

An angry groundswell of support filled the dining room at Bailets' Hotel. From her position on the far side of the room, Ginny could hardly bring herself to look at Nicholas's strained and tired face.

Just as Ginny had feared, the mood of the passengers had turned ugly, strained to the breaking point by the setbacks of the previous day. Instead of a swift and early departure, the trains still sat motionless at Wellington.

The doubleheaded rotary was trapped between two slides to the west. No one even knew the exact location of the eastern rotary. No word of their predicament could be sent to the outside world. The telegraph lines were down.

But the final straw was a thing not even Ginny

could have imagined. As the uncertain nature of the trains' departure had become so clear, the Bailets had been forced to make a drastic decision. There simply weren't enough supplies to feed the train crews and passengers three meals a day. From now on, there would be only two meals a day, breakfast and dinner.

Where once breakfast had been sumptuous flapjacks, eggs, and bacon, now it would be toast and porridge. Any meat there was would be saved for the evening meal. All servings would be strictly portioned.

Disheartening as the rest of yesterday had been, the announcement of food rationing had been the spark that had ignited the powder keg of the passengers' emotions. Though she'd initially been surprised at the heat of the outburst, by now Ginny thought she understood what had caused them.

It was such an easy step to imagine their situation going from two meals a day to one, as the food supply slowly but surely dwindled. If the weather didn't clear soon and no word of their situation reached the outside world, it wouldn't take an avalanche to wipe out the passengers and train crews. They would all simply starve to death in the mountains.

The passengers' fears for their safety had exploded in angry demands. Just as he had when news of the Cascade avalanche had come through, Nicholas was bearing the brunt of them. Superintendent O'Neill was gone once more. Shortly after breakfast, he and several other men had set out on foot in an attempt to reach the depot at Scenic in the hope that the telegraph there was still working.

Scenic marked the end of the hairpin turn the tracks took on the western side of the tunnel, to help the trains lose elevation. It was only a matter of a few miles on foot. But the trains couldn't simply head straight down the mountain. Even for the men, it would be treacherous going. No one knew what the conditions would be like. There was every chance the Superintendent and his men would be unable to reach the depot.

Instead of consoling them, O'Neill's departure had made the passengers even angrier, even edgier. It felt to many as if they'd been abandoned. Shortly after O'Neill's departure, a large group had demanded a meeting with a railroad representative.

Ginny watched as Nicholas turned his head to focus on the man who was demanding that the trains be moved. The movement was stiff, as if just holding his head up required effort.

"Where would you suggest I move them to, sir?" Nicholas asked quietly.

"How dare you?" the man shouted, leaping to his feet. He banged his walking stick upon the floor and Ginny belatedly recognized Judge McAllister. "How dare you patronize me?" the Judge demanded.

Nicholas passed a hand across his face. Even from

across the room, it seemed to Ginny that she could see him visibly working to restrain his temper.

"I beg your pardon, sir," he said, his tone still quiet. "I intended no disrespect, but merely to pose a simple question. You want the trains moved, I understand that. What I cannot seem to impress upon you—upon any of you—" Nicholas raised his voice. His eyes roamed the roomful of angry passengers. "—is that all of us who work for the railroad genuinely believe trains are safest right where they are. There is simply no other place to which I can move them."

"What about up into the snowsheds?" a voice near Ginny demanded.

"Or the tunnel?" asked Mrs. Starling.

"The tunnel is completely out of the question," Nicholas said at once. "It's cold and wet, and would trap the steam and coal smoke. You could all suffocate in a matter of hours."

"Don't heat the cars, then," a third voice called out. "We can take the cold."

Nicholas shook his head emphatically. "I'm sorry," he said. "I cannot run the trains into the tunnel."

"You mean you won't!" the man with the cane said, thumping it once again for emphasis. "We've made a perfectly reasonable request, and you're refusing us."

"Sir," Nicholas said. "I—"

But the other man rode right over him. "Have you looked at that snowfield above the trains?" he shouted. "The slope is completely white from all the snow we've had. The tops of all those dead trees are completely covered over. That whole mountainside is just waiting to come down. It's an avalanche waiting to happen. I say the trains should be moved into the tunnel without delay. And if you're cowardly enough to refuse us, I demand that you put your refusal in writing!"

"Here, here!" voices cried out.

"You should be ashamed of yourselves!"

An astonished silence fell upon the dining room. Then Ginny heard a soft rustle of garments as, one by one, heads turned to stare in the direction of the newcomer. As she realized who it was, she felt her body begin to tingle in shock. It was Virginia who had spoken.

Virginia stood in the doorway between the kitchen and the dining room, her hands on her hips, her hazel eyes sparkling. Her face was flushed an angry red. Ginny had never seen her look so forceful.

"You should be ashamed of yourselves," Virginia said once more. "Nicholas and all the railroad crews have been working day and night to get us out of here. As far as I can make out, all you've done is to complain about your own comfort. The women have helped Mrs. Bailets cook and serve your meals. But the only man of you who's helped do anything at all is Philip Hubbard. If you want something done so much, why don't you stop talking and do it yourselves?"

"With all respect, it's not our job to make sure the trains keep running, ma'am," Judge McAllister answered after a startled moment. "That's the job of the Great Northern. Much as I commend your desire to support your fiancé—"

He broke off as Mrs. Starling began to whisper to him, furiously. "Oh," he said, his head swiveling between Ginny and Virginia. "I beg your pardon, Miss Nolan."

Virginia's face paled and her hands dropped to her sides. Ginny could practically see the fight go right out of her. Her desire to defend Nicholas had been so strong, she'd forgotten that, as far as the other passengers were concerned, she didn't have the right to.

"No one is more concerned for the safety of the trains and passengers than I am, ladies and gentlemen," Nicholas spoke quietly into the strange, strained silence. "*Absolutely no one.* But what I cannot seem to make you understand is that I couldn't move the trains into the tunnel even if thought that was best."

"Why the hell not?" the Judge demanded.

Nicholas's keen eyes shot to his face. At the expression in them, the other man sat down abruptly.

"You say you've looked up at the snowfield," Nicholas said, his quiet voice traveling easily to all corners of the silent dining room. His eyes roamed over the assembled passengers, one by one. "Have you looked beneath your own two feet? Have you looked at the tracks? Can you even find them?

"There's nearly three days worth of accumulated snow on the ground and on the tracks, and I have no way to clear it. Even if I knew for certain that hillside would come down, I couldn't move the trains. *I have no working rotary.*"

As the enormity of what he was saying sank in, Ginny could hear one of the women begin to weep quietly. It was what she felt like doing herself. They were trapped, just as surely as the doubleheader at Windy Point. Stuck fast, with the great snowfield rising straight up above them.

Ginny stared across the room at Nicholas's tired, desperate face. Without warning, she shivered. Goosebumps tingled along the surface of her skin. In her heart, even in the midst of her love, a terrible fear began to blossom.

There was a reason she couldn't see the future, and it had nothing to do with the situation with Virginia. Ginny couldn't see the future because there wasn't going to be one. She was going to lose everything she held dear in this cold, forbidding place.

She was going to die at Wellington.

ॐ 20 ॐ

"Ginny?"

Ginny started at the sound of the familiar voice, but her eyes never left the snowfield.

She'd spent the day on the train helping Claudia Hubbard and the other mothers occupy the restless, fretful children. Since their time on the train was now extended indefinitely, Lucius and the porter on the Similkameen had made the decision to leave about half of each car made up in sleeping berths. That way, the children and older folks could rest if they needed to.

Ginny hadn't seen Virginia since her outburst in defense of Nicholas. She'd tried to speak with her after the tension-filled meeting in the dining room without success. By the time she'd made it across the room, Virginia had vanished.

Ginny was worn out from her long hours in the

close, hot train car, filled with the smells of worried, unwashed bodies, the cries of fussy children. The air in the cars felt thick with fear. Ginny began to fear that she would suffocate.

Finally, just before dinner, an exhausted Claudia and her children had fallen into a troubled sleep. Ginny had returned to the Winnipeg, bundled into her coat, and slipped from the train. Anything was better than staying in the train car, even staring up at the snowfield which threatened them. Standing at the side of her Pullman car, staring upward, Ginny could see that the Judge had been right in his description of it. All traces of the blackened trees had vanished as if they had never existed. The snow above Ginny stretched as pure and white as icing on a wedding cake.

Wedding cake, she thought. No matter which way her mind went, it found only trouble.

"Ginny?" the voice said again. She turned, finally taking her eyes off the snowfield.

"Hello, Nicholas," she said. She wrapped her arms across her chest. It was the only thing that kept her from wrapping them around him. Nicholas looked beyond exhausted. His eyes were red-rimmed, his face chalk-pale.

"How long has it been since you've had any sleep?" Ginny asked.

"I don't think I can remember," Nicholas said

with an attempt at a smile. He moved to stand beside her, his arms at his sides, staring up at the great, white snowfield as if it would help him to gauge her troubled mood. Ginny let her eyes follow his.

"Nicholas," she said, after a moment. "If I ask you something, will you answer me honestly?"

"Of course," he answered at once. "What is it?"

She took her eyes from the snow to watch his face. "Are we going to die here?"

She saw his jaw clench, as if biting down on an unwelcome answer. In the next minute, he'd turned and pulled her to him. "Nothing is going to happen to you, Ginny, I swear. If I thought I was going to lose you I—"

"Don't," she said, pressing trembling fingers against his mouth. "Don't. I shouldn't have asked. It's just—when I try to think about the future . . ." He turned his head, pressing his lips into the center of her palm.

"There's only one thing you need to know," he said. "I love you."

Ginny felt her heart explode within her. She had given up her past, could see no future. The only thing she had was this.

"I love you," she whispered. "I will always love you."

"I thought that you were going to rest."

Startled, Nicholas spun around, his arms dropping. "Miss Nolan!" he said.

Ginny looked past him to where Virginia stood in the snow. Virginia's eyes looked back. They were strangely blank. Ginny couldn't read the expression in them.

"I thought that you were going back to the train to rest," she said again, her eyes softening as they left Ginny to look at Nicholas. "I heard you promise Philip Hubbard."

Nicholas ran a hand across his face, in weariness or embarrassment, Ginny didn't know which. "You're right," he said. "I did. Thank you for coming to my defense this morning," he added.

Virginia blushed. "You're welcome," she said. All of a sudden, she seemed to remember what she'd come for. "Mrs. Bailets sent me with a fresh pillowcase for you," she went on, lifting the piece of bedding she held in her hands. "If you tell me which berth is yours, I'll put it on for you."

"I'm next to the men's washroom on the Similkameen," Nicholas answered automatically. "Lower berth on the right as you walk down the car. You can tell which one is mine because the upper berth isn't made up."

"But what am I thinking?" Nicholas asked suddenly, passing a hand across his face once more. "I couldn't impose like that on you, Miss Nolan. If you'll give me the case, I'll do it myself, but I hope you'll give Mrs. Bailets my thanks for her thoughtfulness."

Virginia stepped forward and handed him the pillowcase, but Ginny was sure she could see her reluctance. She wants to do something for him, she thought. Anything to stake her claim. "I'll do that," Virginia promised.

"I'll go in, then," Nicholas said. "It's cold out here. Don't stay out too long."

He moved swiftly along the path to the train and climbed aboard. Ginny and Virginia were left alone. An awkward silence stretched between them, as great as the snowfield. Ginny had no idea how to reach across it. They'd started out so close together, but each day that had trapped them on the train had driven them farther and farther apart.

"Virginia."

With a fierce gesture of one hand, Virginia cut her off. The expression in her eyes was easy to read now, Ginny thought. Pain. Anger.

"I don't know what you think you're doing," Virginia said in a hard, choked voice. "What you think you feel for Nicholas. It's not important. I only care about one thing."

"What's that?" Ginny asked.

Virginia gave a bark of laughter. The bitterness of it stole Ginny's breath. "You're so clever—don't you know?"

"Virginia," Ginny protested. "Please, it doesn't have to be this way. I never meant to hurt you—for any of this to happen."

"But you're not sorry now that it has, are you?" Virginia challenged. "I may not be outgoing, the way you are, but that doesn't make me blind or stupid. I see what Nicholas feels for you. But he's a good man, Ginny. He deserves better than what you're giving him. He deserves to know the truth."

Ginny felt a heaviness, as if a great stone had come to rest upon her heart. "I know he does," she answered.

"Well, when were you thinking of telling him?" Virginia asked sarcastically. "When the two of you are standing at the altar? 'Oh, by the way, dear, I hope you won't mind if I trade places with Miss Nolan.'"

"Stop it!" Ginny said sharply, finally goaded. "This is as difficult for me as it is for you. It's not fair to blame me, Virginia, and you know it."

"I don't know what's fair anymore," Virginia cried. "All I know is that you're taking him away from me. You're breaking your promise. How is this going to work out all right, Ginny? *How?* Can you tell me that?"

Ginny was silent.

"I didn't think so," Virginia said. "So I'll tell you my plan, Miss Virginia Nolan. If you haven't told

Nicholas the truth by tomorrow morning, then I will."

She turned on her heel, and walked back toward the hotel, leaving Ginny staring after her.

Late that night, Ginny lay in her bunk, gazing up into the darkness. All around her, she could hear the sounds of her fellow passengers. The snores of the men. From time to time, the whimpering of children. She could hear Virginia breathing deeply and evenly just below her. But Ginny didn't think she'd ever get to sleep. Her thoughts moved in the same spiral, over and over.

She hadn't told him.

Much as she'd agreed with Virginia that Nicholas deserved the truth, in the end, Ginny hadn't been able to bring herself to do it. She'd been unable to face the look in his eyes when he discovered who she really was. Unable to face a future without him.

Restlessly, Ginny rolled over onto one side, her eyes fixed on the motionless green curtain. Even with her back to it, it seemed to her that she could feel the vast expanse of the snowfield, rising in silent menace up the mountainside behind her. Instinctively, her fingers reached for the comfort of her mother's ring, then clenched in frustration as she realized Virginia still wore it.

Soon, she would wear another ring. Nicholas's ring.

And Ginny would have nothing.

She shifted position again, pressing her face against her pillow to keep from crying her frustration, her desire, aloud.

If only I could have some token.

Some part of Nicholas that would belong to her—to them—alone. Something that no one could ever take from her. One memory that would burn in her heart for all the empty years to come, brightly enough to warm her for a lifetime.

Ginny threw back the covers, unable to lie still any longer. She knew what she was going to do now, the most impulsive act of her entire life. She was going to go to him. Even if he refused the thing she offered, she'd know she'd acted according to her heart.

The wooden floor of the Winnipeg was icy against Ginny's bare feet, the connecting passage between the two sleeping cars so cold it stole her breath away.

Then, finally, Ginny was standing on the Similkameen beside Nicholas's berth. She took one moment to steady the roaring of her heart, then eased the curtain open.

Tired as he was, the movement roused Nicholas at once. In the dim light, Ginny could just make out his outline as he started up to one elbow. She could see his eyes glittering in the dark.

"Ginny?" she heard him whisper incredulously.

In answer, she stepped forward, leaning down to place one palm over his heart. As she felt the frantic scramble of it, the wild rhythm the exact match for her own, she knew his need matched her own. Knew he understood the thing that had driven her to find him.

"Ginny . . ." He sighed her name out, no more than a breath of sound. Then Ginny felt one strong, sure hand clasp her own, easing her down till they lay heart to heart, while the other pulled the curtain closed, shutting out the world around them.

❧ 21 ❧

The railyard at Wellington
February 28, 1910

"Where were you this morning?"

Ginny was standing on the porch of Bailets' Hotel, watching the rain come down. She'd been waiting for something to happen all morning. Virginia had given her until today to tell Nicholas the truth. Sooner or later, she was bound to seek Ginny out to discover whether or not she'd done it.

Ginny had awakened that morning to the sound of rain on the train car roof, and the warmth of Nicholas's arms around her. Overnight, the weather had changed. The sky was no longer white with snow. Instead, it was filled with enormous, fat drops of rain, shimmering gray as an opal.

After helping to serve breakfast, Ginny had come out onto the hotel porch to watch the rain, listening to it hiss as it struck the snow, the strange booming cracks of sound that echoed from time to time up and down the mountain.

No one seemed to know for sure what caused the sounds, but at breakfast, a word had run through the dining room like wildfire: *avalanche*.

That was the reason she was so jumpy, Ginny told herself. Not Virginia's sudden question. There was no way the other girl could have known where Ginny had spent the night. When Ginny had returned to their berth, it had been early morning. No one on the cars was stirring, not even the porters. Virginia had been lying perfectly still.

"I don't know what you mean," she said. "I've been here all morning just like you have, helping Mrs. Bailets."

Virginia stepped up to stand beside her. Shoulder to shoulder, the two girls stood, staring out into the rain.

"I woke up very early this morning," Virginia said, as if she was telling a bedtime story. "Before it was light. Maybe it was the sound of the rain. Or maybe I was having a nightmare. I woke up frightened. I went to the washroom to splash some water on my face. I thought I'd been careful to keep the curtain closed, so I wouldn't disturb you, but I guess I hadn't. When I got back, the curtain was open."

For the first time, Virginia turned to look at Ginny directly. Almost against her will, Ginny also turned, compelled to meet Virginia's gaze. She'd expected outrage, anger. Instead, she found the other girl's eyes were filled with immeasurable pain. As if she already knew the answer Ginny would give, but had had no choice but to pose the question.

"I could see that you weren't in your bed," Virginia said, her voice still low and quiet. "Where did you go, Ginny? Where were you this morning?"

A thousand images seemed to rush through Ginny's tired mind, a thousand explanations, a thousand choices. Until finally, as there'd been last night, she knew that there was only one choice that she could make.

"I was with Nicholas," she answered.

Virginia gave a cry of anguish. Unable to bear the pain in her friend's eyes another moment, Ginny turned away. She felt Virginia's fingers dig into her shoulders as she reached to pull her back.

"Don't do that," Virginia panted. "Don't think I'm going to let you turn away. You didn't tell him, did you? Instead, you made sure you could keep him for yourself. You knew that was the only way."

"No," Ginny protested. She genuinely hadn't thought of her action in this way. She'd thought only of her need to be with Nicholas. Her need to create something, some memory she could treasure always, through the long and empty years ahead. "It wasn't like that, Virginia."

Virginia began to laugh wildly. "I don't believe you," she said. "You deliberately betrayed him. You deliberately betrayed me. You made sure he had to choose you no matter who you are. You've won. Congratulations."

"What do you mean no matter who she is?" said a voice behind them.

Startled, both girls swung around to face the entrance to the hotel. *No*, Ginny thought, as she stared into Nicholas's horrified blue eyes. *Oh, please, God, no. Not like this.*

"What—do—you—mean—no—matter—who—she—is?" Nicholas asked again, his words carefully spaced out, empty of emotion. But now the expression in his eyes was so blinding, Ginny had to look away. "You aren't Virginia Hightower, are you?" he said, as if the fact that Ginny couldn't look at him had already given him the answer. "You're Virginia Nolan."

"Nicholas, please," Ginny pleaded. "You must believe me, I didn't mean for this to happen. I never meant to hurt either of you."

"I'm not interested in an explanation," Nicholas said, his voice as still as death. "I'm interested in an answer. *Are you Virginia Hightower or Virginia Nolan?*"

Ginny felt her throat close up. She never knew how she forced the words out, the words she knew would send him from her side forever. Her own name.

"Virginia Nolan."

For a fraction of an instant, Nicholas closed his eyes. When he opened them again, Ginny cried out. The fire in them was completely gone. All that was left was cold, blue ashes.

"It was all a lie, wasn't it?" he asked.

"No, Nicholas," Ginny protested, taking a step forward, and felt a pain shoot straight through her heart when he stepped back. "It wasn't a lie, not how I felt, only who I was."

Nicholas gave a bark of cold, harsh laughter. "Only who you were," he said. "And you thought that was unimportant?"

"Of course not," Ginny protested. "I—we—" Her voice faltered and broke off.

"I wanted to know what you were like," Virginia spoke up suddenly, "before we could be married. My father was—not a—kind man. I wanted to make certain you weren't like him, if I could."

"Not a kind man," Nicholas echoed. He gave another short bark of bitter laughter. "But perhaps neither am I, Miss Hightower. A kind man would have told you the truth at once."

Ginny felt Virginia go stone still.

"What truth?" Virginia asked.

"It was such a romantic story, wasn't it?" Nicholas said by way of answer.

Abruptly, Ginny became aware that she was holding her breath. Was this how Nicholas had felt just a few short moments ago? she wondered. As if the world was suddenly descending straight down into chaos.

"The young man who was so eager to meet his fiancée that he boarded the train in the middle of the night rather than wait for her to come to him in Seattle—"

Nicholas's eyes flicked to Ginny for a fraction of a second. "But romantic stories are seldom the truth," he said.

"What is the truth, Nicholas?" Ginny asked. Nicholas's gaze moved back to Virginia.

"I got on the train to tell Miss Hightower that I could not marry her."

Virginia flinched as if she'd been struck, and staggered back. Acting solely on instinct, Ginny moved to support her. Virginia jerked her arm out of her grasp. In the silence that followed, Ginny could hear the sound of the rain, pounding like fists on the roof of the porch.

"But why?" Virginia finally said. Nicholas took a step toward her. Ginny clenched her fists at her side. He had stepped toward Virginia. From her, he'd stepped back.

"My father wished me to promise to marry you," Nicholas said. "He wished to use our marriage to settle a debt he said he owed your father. But I could not agree to that. Marriage should be more than a business contract, Miss Hightower. It should be, as the ceremony says, a promise to love, honor, and protect."

"But you—you said nothing!" Virginia protested.

"Our engagement became common knowledge before I could speak," Nicholas said. "And then—" He broke off, his face coloring.

"Then you met Ginny and realized that you loved her," Virginia filled in slowly. "There would have been no need to speak after that."

When Nicholas said nothing, Virginia suddenly began to laugh. The sound was high-pitched, almost hysterical.

"How miraculous it must have seemed!" Virginia said. "To suddenly discover you loved the woman you'd refused to marry. That's a romantic story, too, Mr. Bennett. Too bad it wasn't the truth."

Ginny watched as the color in Nicholas's face deepened. "I did you a disservice, Miss Hightower," he said. "I'm sorry for it. If you let me, I will make amends."

No! Ginny's heart cried out, even as she felt it spasm in her breast. He could mean just one thing. Before she could stop herself, she took a step forward, one hand extended.

"Don't," Nicholas said. "I don't want you to touch me, Ginny. Not ever again." Ginny felt the words turn her heart to solid ice. She halted, her arm still outstretched.

In a blur of motion, Nicholas actually knelt on the porch before Virginia. "Will you do me the honor of becoming my wife, Miss Hightower?"

Virginia looked down, her expression unreadable. "Yes, I will, Mr. Bennett," she answered at last.

As if Virginia's answer had freed her from some spell, Ginny dropped her hand. She knew it rested against her leg. She could even see her fingers curl to grasp the dark fabric of her heavy skirt. But she couldn't feel the ache of muscles clenching till her knuckles shone white.

She couldn't feel anything, would never feel anything, not ever again.

"We can be married as soon as we reach Seattle," Nicholas said, rising to take Virginia's hand.

Ginny turned away, no longer able to bear the sight of Nicholas and Virginia together. She stared out over the snow, lumpy and pock-marked by the falling rain. A huge *crack* thundered through the valley.

"But first, I have to make the hike to Scenic," she heard Nicholas continue. "Bailets is almost out of supplies, and I need to see if I can arrange for more."

"But is that safe, Nicholas?" Virginia asked anxiously.

How quick she is to voice her fears for him, Ginny thought. *Almost as if they're married already.*

"It will be all right," Nicholas reassured her. "But before I go—I—there is some—business—I must finish with Miss Nolan."

"Do you want me to go inside?" Virginia asked.

There was a beat of silence.

"You are going to be my wife," Nicholas answered slowly. "There should be no secrets between us, though I fear you may not like what you will hear."

"I already know about last night," Virginia told him.

Ginny felt something sharp and ugly twist inside her. *So this is what betrayal feels like,* she thought.

"Miss Nolan."

Nicholas's voice sliced through Ginny's bitter consciousness. Slowly, she turned to face him, trying to focus just on him, and not on Virginia at all.

For what she was sure was the last time, Ginny felt Nicholas's eyes upon her. Now they reminded her even more of a winter sky: a blue so pure and bleak it made her own eyes water. And so cold, even the memory of warmth was gone.

"If you should discover that—what we . . . that you are . . ."

"Don't," Ginny whispered. "Please, don't."

"I want you to know that you will be provided for," Nicholas said haltingly.

How could she have been so blind? So stupid? In her need for something to cherish, she had never stopped to consider that she and Nicholas could create a child between them. A child that would be nothing more to him than Ginny had been to Stephen and Amanda: an obligation, a burden.

"But, unless you discover you're carrying my child, I never want to see or hear from you again, Miss Nolan. I can't—"

Abruptly, he broke off, his lips pressed tightly together. Without warning, he brushed between Ginny and Virginia, stepping down off the porch and striding off into the driving rain.

It's over, Ginny thought. *All, all over.* She felt exhausted, drained. She turned to Virginia, standing silently beside her on the porch.

"It seems that you are the one to be congratulated. I'm sure you'll be very happy."

"But not Nicholas," Virginia answered sharply. "Not without you—is that what you mean?"

Ginny bit down on her tongue until she tasted blood. Things were bad enough. She would not add to them by further quarreling.

"I won't stay on the Winnipeg," she went on when she could trust herself to speak. "I don't expect you'll want to bunk with me anymore. I'll move to the Similkameen."

"You know where there's an empty berth," Virginia answered. Then she made a swift gesture, as if to call her harsh words back. "Well, at least we were right about one thing."

"What's that?"

"We were right about the kind of man Nicholas Bennett is. He's good and honorable. So honorable he's willing to live without love."

Without another word, Virginia turned and went back into the hotel. Ginny walked slowly down the steps and out onto the snow, lifting her tear-stained face to the bitter rain.

❦ 22 ❦

All that day and into the night, it rained. Huge, fat drops falling from the sky like a torrent of tears, pelting down upon the trains and the buildings, soaking into the dense-packed snowfields, turning the sky no longer white, but a strange and opalescent gray.

Toward the middle of the night, as February faded away and March roared in like a lion, the thunder and lightning began. Great claps of sound hurled themselves from one side of the canyon to the other. Silver forks of lightning seared the sky. Illuminated by their light, the great, white snowfield seemed to hold its breath.

Then, in the beat of stillness that followed the thunder, there came a sound no one had ever heard before.

A sound like nothing anyone had ever imagined,

not even in the depths of their most fevered nightmares. A wild beast's roar. A sound to end all other sounds on earth, to swallow them up, to drown them out, to crush them and destroy them.

The great, white snowfield above the trains was moving. The avalanche came down.

Ginny heard it first, a great roar filling the night, making any other sound impossible. Ginny's head shot up from her pillow. She twisted her neck from side to side, trying in vain to identify the sound's direction.

And then the avalanche was upon her.

Ginny screamed as she felt the Similkameen lift up, up, up, slamming her brutally against the top of the train, then, with a force hard enough to break bone, crash her right back down again. Crying out in fear and pain, she tumbled over the side of her berth, her hands desperately scrabbling for any kind of hold as the Pullman car began to spin around like a toy boat trapped in a whirlpool.

Ginny's ears were filled with an assault of sound. The sound of glass breaking as snow forced its way through the windows, the scrape of rocks and trees sliding along the sides of the car, the screams of her fellow passengers. She saw a strange glow, like red hot stars, and realized the coal stove had tipped over.

A shape slid toward her along the floor. Instinctively, Ginny made a quick grab, astonished to discover it was Abigail Hubbard. With one arm, Ginny hugged the baby to her chest.

"Claudia!" she screamed out. *"Claudia!"*

"Ginny!" she heard Claudia call back. "I've lost Abby! Where are you?"

"Here!" Ginny called out. "Over here!"

Then the whole world exploded.

Ginny could feel herself hurtle straight up, flying through the air, as the Similkameen split open like a ripe summer melon. For one incredible moment, she seemed to hang above the earth, clutching Abigail Hubbard in her arms, suspended in time and space. Then, with a speed so brutal it stole her breath, she began to plummet downward.

She felt a sudden, piercing cold, a shooting pain. Then she could see nothing. Hear nothing. Feel nothing.

I'm going to die here, she thought. Then she remembered nothing.

❦ 23 ❦

Ginny came to her senses slowly, opening first one eye, and then the other. But even with her eyes open, the world refused to make sense.

Why is it so cold? she wondered. *Amanda hates it when the house is cold. . . .*

But you left Amanda, her mind answered. *You left Stephen.*

Oh, yes, she thought. *I remember. I ran away. I went to the train depot. There was a girl on the train—and someone else—*

Nicholas!

With a sharp spear of pain, all Ginny's senses sharpened. She knew where she was now. She was lying, face down, in the aftermath of the avalanche, one arm pinned beneath her stomach, the other outflung. She could feel the fabric of her nightdress against her forehead. Her face lay in the crook of

215

her outstretched arm. All around her, she could feel the cold, wet press of the snow.

I'm not in the train anymore, she thought. *I'm buried, buried in the snow.* She was completely covered, though by some miracle she'd been buried with an air pocket. She could breathe, but she wasn't sure yet that she could move. She could feel a great weight pressing down against her back.

Abby, she thought. *Where is Abby Hubbard?*

Ginny tried to move, then screamed in agony as searing pain shot from her back straight down both legs. She had no idea what held her down, but she was very much afraid that it would hold her there forever. The only thing she could move were the fingers of her outstretched hand. Everything else was useless, motionless, pinned down by some enormous weight.

Ginny stared at her fingers, wriggling uselessly. Her skin looked pinched and bloodless, almost as white as the snow. The cold was so immense it shut out every other sensation but pain.

How long? Ginny wondered. *How long could she survive like this, with nothing between her and the snow?*

And where was the Hubbard's baby? Had she slipped from Ginny's grip on impact?

"Abby," she whispered. Ginny held her breath. Gradually, from the hollow just below her stomach, she became aware of a tiny thread of sound: Abigail Hubbard's breathing.

I've got to reach her, Ginny thought. *Got to keep her warm.* She tried to move the arm pinned beneath her, but it was useless. She couldn't feel it anymore. Hot tears scalded Ginny's freezing cheeks as she realized the truth. Abigail Hubbard was right beneath her, but Ginny couldn't reach her. She could offer her no shelter, no protecting warmth. Abby's life depended on Ginny now, and she could do nothing to save it. Just as she could do nothing to save her own.

All she could do was to pray. Pray that she and Abby weren't the only ones left alive on earth. Pray that somewhere, someone was mounting a rescue, that they would get to them in time.

"It's all right. I'm here, Abby," Ginny said. "Shall I sing you a lullaby? I'll sing you a lullaby," she babbled. "Hush, little baby, don't say a word . . ."

Over and over, Ginny sang the same song. She never knew how long. She sang till her voice gave out and only her lips kept moving. Till the only sounds in her coffin of snow were her own heart beat and Abigail Hubbard's whispery rasps.

In and out. In and out, Ginny forced the air into her own aching lungs, as if every breath she took somehow gave Abby breath. With every inhalation, Ginny felt the weight against her back, pressing her down into the snow. With every exhalation, she felt the cold seep deeper and deeper into her tired body.

Until finally, she was so cold she couldn't feel anything at all, not even the pain, and the only thing she could hear was her own breathing.

She's gone. They're all gone, she thought. *Abby. Nicholas. Virginia.* Praying hadn't done any good. No one had come to save her.

And so, when the miracle finally occurred, Ginny almost didn't recognize it, she'd been so certain it would never happen. She heard a strange sound, the ring of metal shovels against the snow.

"I think we're just about done with this spot, boys," she heard a voice say.

"No, I'm here," Ginny murmured, a tiny spark of warmth, the will to live, suddenly flaring to life within her. She tried to lift her head. Pain shot like a hot poker down her back. Ginny cried out.

"Wait a minute," a second voice said. "I thought I heard something. Is anybody there? Can anybody hear my voice?"

"I'm here," Ginny called back, her voice stronger this time. "I'm here! Help me!"

"My God, there is someone," the first voice agreed. "Be careful, now. Don't dig too deep too fast."

Ginny heard the ring of shovels all around her. A moment later, she felt cold, fresh air upon the back of her head.

"It's a woman," she heard the voice exclaim. "It looks like Miss Hightower. Where's Nicholas Bennett? Somebody tell him I think we've found his fiancée."

"Nicholas," Ginny said. Then she tumbled into darkness.

✣ 24 ✣

The railyard at Wellington
Early March 1910

She was freezing. She was burning. She didn't know where she was, or where she'd been. The surface of Ginny's skin felt scorched with fever. But inside, she was as cold as the snow and ice she'd been so sure would be her grave. So cold she feared she could never be warm again.

She could feel hands upon her, barely make out the shapes of people around her, their voices low and soothing as they spoke her name.

"You must stay still, Miss Hightower," they told her, over and over. "Lie still. You have to rest."

"Abby," she thought she'd whispered. "Claudia. Virginia. Nicholas."

And then at last, one shape had detached itself from the others, one outline that was clearer than the rest.

"It's all right, I'm here, Ginny."

"Nicholas," Ginny said again. She reached up, to where the figure stood above the bed. "You have to find Nicholas and ask him something for me."

"What is it?" the figure said. But Ginny's strength was failing, her vision growing dim. "What is it?" the figure said again, leaning closer, until its form blocked out everything else.

From the depths of her freezing heart, Ginny summoned her last ounce of strength. "Ask him to forgive me," she whispered.

The next time she awoke, Nicholas was sitting by the side of her bed.

He was asleep in a wooden chair the exact match for the ones in the dining room at the Bailets' Hotel, his head dropped forward onto his chest. At his side was a table with a pitcher of water and one of Mrs. Bailets' green plants.

Is this real or am I still delirious, imagining things? Ginny wondered.

"Nicholas?" she whispered.

At once, Nicholas's eyes opened, their piercing blue turning toward the bed. For a silence Ginny had no way to measure, they stared at one another. Ginny couldn't tell what he was feeling. The dead, flat expression was gone from his eyes, but in its place was something she'd never seen before, something she didn't understand.

"I'm thirsty," she murmured.

At once Nicholas rose and poured her a glass of water. "You've had a fever," he answered. "You've been delirious for more than a week." He moved to the bed, helped prop her up so she could drink, then handed her the glass and stepped back.

He doesn't want to touch me, Ginny thought. *Not any more than he has to.* She couldn't blame him. The last time they'd touched had meant betrayal for them both. She drank the water in slow sips, grateful for its cool slide down her parched throat.

"It's a miracle that you're alive at all," Nicholas continued, as he sat down again. "You were buried in the snow for nearly eleven hours with one of the biggest tree trunks I've ever seen pressed against your back. Why your back and legs aren't broken, I'll never know."

The glass wobbled in Ginny's grasp as memory poured through her. "Abby . . . ?"

His eyes filled with sympathy, Nicholas shook his head. "The rest of the Hubbards are alive, though. Philip's collarbone is broken. Claudia has a big gash on her forehead, but Thomas came through without a scratch. They've gone on to Seattle, but Claudia asked me to tell you she hoped they'd see you there, and that . . . she knew you'd done your best."

Ginny closed her eyes against the tears that rose

and threatened to spill over. How could Claudia be so compassionate, so forgiving?

"I couldn't get to her," she whispered, opening her eyes. "All I could do was wiggle my fingers. I couldn't move my arms or legs."

"Nobody could have expected you to do anything more, Ginny."

"But, if she'd been with Claudia—" Ginny began. Without warning, a familiar head poked in through the curtained doorway.

"Oh, so she's awake at last," Mrs. Bailets said. "I'll tell the doctor. He'll be so pleased. Now you concentrate on getting your strength back, young lady."

From somewhere, Ginny summoned up the strength to smile. "You just want some help in the kitchen."

"There now," Mrs. Bailets pounced, as if Ginny had just helped her win an argument. "What did I tell you? Soon, she'll be just as healthy as that plant," she said. Her head disappeared, and Ginny could hear the sound of her brisk footsteps.

"Damn!"

Ginny's jaw dropped open. She stared at Nicholas. She'd never heard him swear, not even in the heat of his anger over her deception. "I thought you liked Mrs. Bailets," she said.

"I do," Nicholas answered. "But once she tells the doctor you're awake—" He regarded her in silence for a moment, as if gauging her strength. "There's something else you need to know, Ginny. I was going to wait to tell you, but I'm afraid Mrs. Bailets has forced my hand."

"It's about Virginia, isn't it?" Ginny said in a low voice. When Nicholas didn't answer, she knew the truth, forced herself to say the words aloud. "She's dead."

"None of the other passengers on the Winnipeg made it," Nicholas said softly. "I don't know how you did."

So this was what had saved her, Ginny thought. One small twist of fate.

"I wasn't on the Winnipeg," she confessed. "After you left, Virginia and I decided we couldn't bunk together anymore. I moved to the Similkameen." She fell silent, unwilling to tell him she'd slept in the berth they'd shared. "I—"

"Stephen Banks is here," Nicholas said.

The glass slipped from Ginny's fingers as she jerked upright. Water splashed across the bed.

"You mustn't let him see me," she said urgently. The glass crashed to the floor beside the bed.

"But—" Nicholas began.

"Nicholas, please, listen to me," Ginny pleaded. What could she do to make him understand?

"I know you no longer—care for me—" her voice stumbled, but she forced herself to go on. "But, *please*, don't tell Stephen Banks I'm here. I can't go back to Spokane. If all you're going to do is turn me over to him, you should have left me to die in the snow."

Heedless of the broken glass upon the floor, Nicholas moved to the side of the bed. His fingers reached for Ginny's chin, holding her head perfectly still. For one long moment, he looked down into her eyes.

"You're serious, aren't you?"

"Dead serious," Ginny said. "Even if you hate me, don't tell him I'm here. Please, Nicholas, I beg—"

"Well, get in there and ask Bennett when I *can* see her!" a voice just outside the doorway said. "I can't stay here forever. I'm a busy man."

Ginny jerked her head out of Nicholas's grasp. She had to get away, any way she could. Desperately, her hands fumbled for the covers.

"Stay still, Ginny," Nicholas said. Without another word, he turned toward the doorway. In two long strides he was through it, drawing the curtain shut behind him.

"What do you want, Banks?" he said.

"The same thing I've wanted for the last week," Stephen Banks's angry voice said. "I have questions concerning my stepsister. I think your fiancée may be able to answer them. I hear she's awake. All I want to do is talk to her, Bennett."

A wave of shock passed through Ginny. She

pressed her hands to her mouth to keep her emotions back. All this time, Nicholas had been protecting her, and she hadn't known it. He hadn't allowed Stephen to see her, hadn't revealed the identity switch. Only Nicholas and Ginny knew the truth about the Ginny Nolan who lay buried under who knew how many feet of snow, knew that she was really Virginia Hightower. But Stephen Banks didn't know it.

Her stepbrother believed that she was dead!

"I have told you, Miss Hightower has nothing to tell you," Nicholas answered, his next words confirming Ginny's realization. "She's weak, recovering from an ordeal you can't begin to imagine. She cannot be disturbed. I will not allow it."

"But, my stepsister's belongings," Stephen protested.

He's talking about my mother's jewelry, Ginny realized suddenly. Stephen and Amanda must have searched her room, realized what she had taken. She had no idea where her coat was, no doubt buried beneath the snow.

"Your stepsister's *belongings?*" Nicholas said. Ginny felt the hairs on the back of her neck stand on end. She had never heard Nicholas's voice sound like this, not even when he'd faced down a roomful of angry passengers. "That's all that really concerns you, isn't it?" he asked.

"You don't care about finding her body. You don't

care that the only way we had to identify Miss Nolan was by the ring on her right hand. Her *severed* right hand, Mr. Banks. That's all we have of your stepsister. All we may have till spring. I suggest you return to look for her *belongings* then."

A wave of nausea flooded through Ginny. *Dear God*, she thought. Virginia hadn't deserved such a fate. No one did. She drew her knees up and hugged them to her chest.

"Your behavior is insulting," Stephen blustered. "I intend to lodge a protest with Superintendent O'Neill."

"Fine," Nicholas said promptly. "You do that. In the meantime, leave Miss Hightower alone, or I promise you that you'll regret it."

A moment later, Ginny heard the angry retreat of Stephen's footsteps. Nicholas stepped back through the curtain and held it closed behind him. He pulled in a deep, slow breath. Slowly, Ginny slid her legs down and sat up as straight as she could, staring across the room at him.

"Why did you protect me?" she whispered. "You don't even know my reasons."

"I don't need to know them," Nicholas said. "I have reasons of my own."

Ginny held her breath. Nicholas all but vibrated with tension. He was wound as tightly as a watch spring. But when he spoke once more, his voice was low and controlled. His eyes looked straight ahead, as if he were staring at the past.

"When I left here—that day—I thought I never wanted to see you again. I told myself that offering to marry Virginia was the right thing to do, the honorable thing to do, and that's why I'd acted the way I had."

He paused and, in that moment, Ginny could see the deep lines of weariness etched around his eyes and mouth. *You don't have to do this*, she wanted to say. *You don't have to explain.* But she couldn't seem to force the words out.

Without warning, his blue eyes turned to hers and Ginny felt a jolt. They were haunted, tortured. Had she done that?

"It wasn't true, Ginny," Nicholas burst out, as if the spring inside him had suddenly given way. "I wasn't trying to do the right thing. All I was doing was trying to hurt you—to pay you back. I wanted you to suffer. I wanted you to feel the way I did—betrayed. Then we got word of the avalanche and I—"

He broke off, breathing hard, and turned away. Ginny watched him run a hand across his face, as if to scrub it clean of his unwholesome visions. She was shocked to see that his hand was trembling.

"I thought that I'd go crazy. All I could think about was you. Seeing you again, holding you again. *I would have given anything to make that happen, Ginny.*

"I didn't give a damn about who you were, all I wanted was to have you back again. I don't know if I can ever forgive the choice you made—coming to me without telling me who you really were—but I think that, now, I can understand it. When I thought I'd lost you, I thought I'd lost everything—except my memories."

Ginny was still for a moment, listening to the steady beat of her own heart and to Nicholas's ragged breathing. He did understand, she thought. Maybe better than she had herself. Her need to build a memory. As much as desire, that was the thing that had pulled her to him that night. But if he couldn't forgive her, a memory would be all they'd ever have.

Ginny never knew how she found the courage to speak. "What happens now?" she asked.

Nicholas ran his hand across his face once more, then turned to face her. Now Ginny saw that his eyes were dim and troubled, as if the fire in them had begun to smoulder but hadn't yet found the way to burst to life.

"I honestly don't know," Nicholas admitted softly. "Part of me still wants to blame you, Ginny. You lied to me. You hurt me, and I responded in a way that I'm not proud of. But if I'd been honest from the start—if I'd told the truth and said I couldn't marry Virginia Hightower, things might

229

have been different. You and I could have been free to love one another. My head knows I have to let go of the past—but my heart—"

"It's still all around us, isn't it?" Ginny whispered. She thought of Virginia, lying cold and dead in the snow. Cold and dead in what could have been her place. Would Virginia's tomb house her own heart? Ginny wondered. Would she be doomed to live alone, without love, in atonement for Virginia's fate?

"Now that I know you will recover, I must leave for Seattle. I can't put it off any longer," Nicholas continued. He came to stand beside the bed. "Perhaps, all we need is time, Ginny. Perhaps—"

Ginny reached for his hand, curving her fingers around his. "What do you want to do?" she asked.

The question burned her throat, it sounded so unlike her. The old Ginny Nolan didn't ask. She made up her mind and then she acted. Without her impetuosity, she never would have met Nicholas Bennett, known his love.

Because of her impetuosity, she might very well have lost his love forever.

I've been no better than Stephen is, Ginny realized suddenly. *Manipulating people, using them to satisfy my own ends*. The knowledge filled her with self-loathing. The fact that she hadn't intended to act in such a fashion hardly made a difference. How could she expect him to love her when she couldn't love herself?

Her fingers slipped from Nicholas's and fell back upon the bed. When Nicholas reached to capture them again Ginny felt her heart stutter.

Perhaps he wasn't ready to let her go. Not yet.

"This is what I think we should do," he answered slowly, gazing down at their joined hands. "I'll hike out to Scenic and take the train back to Seattle. You stay here and recover your strength. When you're ready to travel, if you still . . . want me, wire me when you'll arrive. If I want us to be together, I'll meet you at the train depot."

"And if you're not there?" Ginny asked.

"Then you'll have my answer," Nicholas said. "Just as I'll have yours if you never come to Seattle. We're even now, Ginny. No more lies between us, no more secrets. Both of us must take the same chance."

The chance that, even as one of them moved forward, the other would step back. Ginny felt her heart accelerate with fear at just the thought. She'd been impetuous all her life, but had she ever truly been brave? Was she brave enough to take this chance?

To show by her actions that she wanted Nicholas's love, before she could know if it was still returned?

I am brave enough, she thought. *I must be.*

"All right, Nicholas," she said.

A look of relief swept across Nicholas's face. "Thank you," he said. For a moment, he stood silent, as if, now that he had leave to go, he was uncertain how to do it. Finally, he raised Ginny's hand, still clasped in his own, and pressed it to his lips. Ginny felt the tears start, unbidden, in her eyes. She blinked frantically, desperately trying to hold them back.

She would not weep. Not when it felt so much like giving in to defeat before she'd had the chance to prove that she could win.

"Rest well," Nicholas said. "I hope—"

He broke off abruptly. Without another word, he released her hand and strode away from the bed. At the doorway, he slid the curtain back, stepped through, then slid it into place behind him. Not once did he look back. Ginny heard his quick footsteps walk away from her room, then fade away to nothingness.

Ginny sat in bed, staring at the bright green leaves of Mrs. Bailets's plant. It looked so eager for life, so hopeful, and Ginny had never felt so hopeless.

How much of her heart had just vanished with Nicholas? she wondered. And how much of it would stay forever here in Wellington, buried in the cold among the dead?

❧ 25 ❧

The railyard at Wellington
Late March 1910

"Are you ready to go, Ginny?"

Several weeks later Ginny stood once more on the porch of Bailets' Hotel. This time, she was waiting to board the train that would take her on the final leg of the journey she'd started so long ago, through the mountains to Seattle. She'd been ready to travel for more than a week, but had been forced to stay in the mountains until the tracks could be cleared from Scenic to Wellington.

Both places had been sites of desperate activity during the weeks of Ginny's recovery. Even though they'd had to hike in on foot, rescue crews had poured from Scenic into Wellington. The passenger cars had been dug out first, then below them, the mail cars, all still carrying their loads of human cargo.

It had seemed to Ginny that the sleds carrying

the bodies from the wreckage to the makeshift morgue near the hotel would never stop. To keep herself occupied, she'd helped Mrs. Bailets in the kitchen once more, helping to feed the rescue crews. She'd been glad to keep busy but, more often than not, her appearance proved awkward. Entire tables of men would fall silent at her approach. They knew she was one of the survivors, and they'd all heard about her ordeal.

But it was from overhearing talk at the tables that Ginny learned the fate of the Starlings. Some of the bodies pulled from the wreckage were mangled almost beyond recognition, but not them. They appeared virtually untouched, as if they'd simply fallen asleep under a vast blanket of snow. William had been clasped tightly in his mother's arms. She'd protected him to the very last.

As was the case with all the others, their bodies were loaded onto enormous sleds and hauled out to Scenic, the closest place where the trains were still running.

It was from a compassionate Mrs. Bailets that Ginny had learned Virginia's fate. She'd been entwined with the twisted metal wreckage of the Winnipeg. Only the fact that one of her hands was severed at the wrist had made it possible to identify her. Her face had been crushed beyond recognition.

Ginny's secret was well and truly safe now. It could not be given away, not even by the dead.

In spite of Ginny's pleading, Mrs. Bailets had refused to let her see the body. There was no point in Ginny torturing herself, she said. Virginia was gone. Nothing Ginny could ever do would bring her back.

She'd meant the words as comfort, Ginny knew, but instead she felt guilt settle over her, like a great, dark cloak. What had the woman said who'd first come to congratulate Mr. Bennett and Miss Hightower on their romantic engagement?

The heart always knows its choice.

And because Ginny's heart had chosen Virginia's fiancé, and his heart had chosen her, Ginny was alive and Virginia was dead. And because her friend was dead, Ginny would be free to leave her old life behind forever, if only she had courage enough to take the first step.

A step that felt much larger than the one that had taken her away from Stephen and her life in Spokane. *I was running away then*, Ginny thought. Now, she was running toward. A leap of faith which she must make without a safety net.

"Ginny—" a quiet voice said.

Ginny started and turned. Then she gave a quick, self-conscious laugh. Mrs. Bailets had been there the whole time, she realized suddenly. Had even spoken to her once before, but Ginny had been too lost in her own comfortless thoughts to answer her.

She pulled in a deep breath. Now that the time to leave Wellington had come, Ginny felt awkward and uncertain. Without Mrs. Bailets's support, Ginny was sure she never would have made it through the dark days after Nicholas's departure.

She managed a smile, determined to show the older woman good spirits. "Ready as I'll ever be," she said.

Mrs. Bailets was quiet for a moment, gazing out toward the tracks. The day was cold and clear. Sunlight sparkled like diamonds on the surface of the hard-packed snow.

"Did you wire Nicholas?" Mrs. Bailets asked.

Ginny nodded, unable to trust herself to speak.

"I gave him a piece of my mind before he left, you know," the other woman said.

"You did *what?*" Ginny asked.

Mrs. Bailets chuckled, as if Ginny's startled reaction was exactly what she'd hoped for. "I gave him a piece of my mind," she said again. "I don't know what's gone wrong between you two, but it's nothing that can't be cured by a little forgiveness. That's what I told him—and what I'm telling you."

But you can't know that for certain, Ginny thought. *Just as she couldn't know for certain that he'd be waiting for her at the other end.*

"I'm not sure he can forgive me," she said aloud.

Mrs. Bailets snorted. "Don't be ridiculous. Of course he can," she said. "But he's got to forgive himself first, same as you've got to forgive yourself. All the rest will follow after that."

Ginny felt her heart twist. "You make it sound so simple."

Mrs. Bailets turned to her, her expression ever so slightly surprised. "Well, I think it is," she answered. "But simple's not the same as easy."

"No, it isn't," Ginny said. She took a breath. She thought of Virginia, crushed beyond recognition in the snow. "I—I'm not sure I can forgive myself."

Mrs. Bailets expression turned compassionate. "But I think you must, my dear," she said. "Otherwise, how will you go on?"

Ginny looked back out over the snow, telling herself that her eyes burned because the sunlight was so dazzling.

"I don't know," she said.

Without warning, Mrs. Bailets handed Ginny a basket. It was covered with a red and white checked cloth, bright and cheery. "I fixed a little something for you," the older woman said. "A person should never go on a journey empty handed. Besides, I wanted to thank you for all your help."

"It's I who should thank you," Ginny said,

grateful for the change of subject. "It helped to keep busy."

The other woman nodded, as if she understood. "It's a good feeling to be useful, isn't it?" she commented.

The train let out a long, high whistle.

"Oh, there you go. Better get on board," Mrs. Bailets said. She reached to give Ginny a warm embrace. "Good luck, Ginny."

"And to you," Ginny said. She returned Mrs. Bailets's embrace, then tucked the basket more firmly into the crook of her arm and strode down the porch steps without looking back. The snow scrunched and squeaked as Ginny walked across it. For the last time, she walked toward the tracks at Wellington, the plume of steam from the great black engine shooting like a white geyser into the cold, blue air.

Just before she boarded the train, she stopped and turned in a slow circle. High above where the train now sat, the avalanche had left a jagged scar upon the land, wide and deep, like the scar in Ginny's heart. Who knew how long it would take the land to heal?

But I must be like the earth is, Ginny realized suddenly. She must be strong. She must be patient and relentless. She must commit herself to the future, not the past. Her dream of love had been born, and it had died, in this place. But it could rise once more, reborn by the power of forgiveness.

She swung up into the train, settled into the day car, and set her basket at her feet. No sooner had she done so than she felt the train jerk forward. The future seemed to hurtle toward her as the train gathered speed. Ginny felt her heart lift and open.

There was pain there, pain for her own deception. Pain for the senseless loss of Virginia. Perhaps it would be there always. But pain was not enough to grow a future.

Please, Ginny thought, as she watched Wellington disappear forever. *Please, be there, Nicholas.*

❧ 26 ❧

Seattle, Washington
Late March 1910

She couldn't find him anywhere.

Ginny stood outside the depot in Seattle, her heart pounding in her throat, fingers laced tightly together. Only a supreme act of will was keeping her from wringing her hands. She'd watched the other passengers disembark, be greeted by their loved ones and depart, despair growing in her heart moment by moment, until now she stood all alone beside the great black engine.

It was warmer in Seattle than it was in the mountains, but Ginny was cold, so cold she didn't think she'd ever be warm again. She had made her choice, sending the telegram that showed she wanted a future with Nicholas.

And, in his absence, she had his answer. He didn't want her. Didn't want a life together.

He wasn't coming. She couldn't find him anywhere.

All of a sudden, Ginny simply couldn't stand it. *Go! Get moving!* she told herself. *You can't stand around all night at the train depot.*

But her legs felt slow and clumsy inside their cocoon of petticoats and skirts. As if her body was unwilling to move toward the future, preferring to stay rooted in the past. No matter how painful it had been, in this moment Ginny was sure the pain of the past would be nothing compared to that of the future.

He wasn't coming. She was going to have to learn to live without him.

"Excuse me, miss—"

At the sound of the voice behind her, Ginny turned to find the train conductor hurrying along beside the tracks. In one hand, he held the basket Mrs. Bailets had given Ginny.

"I think you may have left this behind, miss," the conductor said.

"I did—thank you for noticing," Ginny said. She'd been in such a hurry to find Nicholas, she'd forgotten all about Mrs. Bailets's gift. She took the basket, settling it into the crook of one arm.

"Thank you," she said again.

The conductor touched one hand to the brim of his cap. "Think nothing of it, ma'am," he said.

"Evening, sir," he went on, moving on toward the depot.

Ginny spun around, the basket flying out from her elbow as she swiftly turned. She heard a grunt as it connected.

"Whoa—be careful!" a voice exclaimed.

Ginny stopped dead. All she could do was to stare upward into a pair of bright blue eyes she'd been so sure she'd never see again.

"Nicholas," she said. She swayed as her legs, so unwilling to move a moment before, now threatened to stop holding her up. Nicholas reached to hold her at once, his hands grasping both her elbows in a tight, firm grip.

"I was delayed. I couldn't help it, Ginny."

"I thought you weren't coming," Ginny said. She wanted to call the words back the moment she said them. But she'd been so cold, so terribly cold and alone and afraid.

Nicholas winced. "I know—I'm sorry—I—I'm not making a very good start of this, am I?" he said.

Do something, Ginny told herself. *You've come so far, had so many misunderstandings. Don't let one last one ruin things now.*

"What's that?" Nicholas asked suddenly. Ginny followed his gaze to where Mrs. Bailets' basket still dangled from the crook of one of her elbows.

"Mrs. Bailets gave it to me, just before I left," she

242

said. "Probably just food for the trip. I didn't even look—I wasn't hungry—"

"No," Nicholas said, his expression intent. "No, I don't think so. Look, Ginny."

He released one of her elbows to ease the checked cloth back. From the depths of the basket, Ginny could see glossy green leaves. Mrs. Bailets had given her one of her plants, the one that had cheered her from the table by her sickbed.

Ginny felt her body begin to tingle. Felt the rush of her blood, just beneath the surface of her skin. Mrs. Bailets had given her something strong and alive, yet that nevertheless must be tended carefully.

Like my love for Nicholas, Ginny thought. *Like the life we want to build together.*

She looked up to find him watching her intently, his blue eyes burning with the thing Ginny'd feared she'd put out forever: a strong and steady flame. Ginny felt the ice around her heart melt and dissolve away as if it had never been there. She was warm once again.

"Ginny—I—" Nicholas started. Ginny placed gentle fingertips against his lips to silence him.

"I love you, Nicholas," she said. "My heart always knew that you would come—only my fear made me doubt. I'll never listen to it again."

Nicholas made a strangled sound and lowered his forehead to rest against hers. "I was so afraid you wouldn't come," he confessed. "Ten times a day, I told myself I was a fool for leaving you. I don't want to live without you—not for one minute longer. Will you marry me, Ginny?"

"Yes, I will," Ginny said.

Nicholas gave a great whoop and lifted her off her feet, spinning her until they were both breathless and laughing. Then he set her on her feet, took her face between his hands, and kissed her until the sounds of the depot dropped away and all she could hear was the beat of his heart and hers, together.

Hand in hand, they walked to the hansom that would take them to Nicholas's home, and his waiting parents. Safe in the cab, in the shelter of Nicholas's arms, Ginny touched the plant Mrs. Bailets had given her with gentle fingers.

The winter had been long and bitter, and Ginny knew she would never forget it. But now, in the blossoming of the love she shared with Nicholas, Ginny also knew that she would see the spring.

Author's Note

If you were to look at a contemporary map of Washington State, you would find no mention of a place called Wellington. Not long after the lethal avalanche took place, the Great Northern Railway changed the name of the railyard to Tye (tie-ee), no doubt hoping to erase the name of Wellington, and the catastrophe which happened there, from public memory.

It probably didn't do much good in the short run—the disaster was one of the worst in state history. But, in the long run, it seems to have done the trick. I live in Seattle, yet when I told people the subject of my story, almost no one had heard of the events on which this book is based.

The railroad also took other actions as the direct result of the events of 1910, all of them aimed at making certain such a disaster never happened again. They built new snowsheds to cover the tracks, including one 3900 feet long, made of reinforced concrete, on the ledge where the doomed trains had once sat. In the following years, the trouble spot at Windy Point was tunneled through.

Eventually, however, none of it proved enough. The winter passes continued to be so difficult to maintain that, in the end, the Great Northern decided there was only one thing to do: build a new tunnel at a lower elevation. Five hundred feet lower than the one in this story, the new tunnel eliminated the dangerous upper areas entirely. It opened in 1929 and is still in use today. With its opening, the railyard at Wellington/Tye was abandoned.

As was the case with my first book for this series, *Hindenburg, 1937,* the framework for the story, the long, frustrating delays which led up to the final, early morning catastrophe, actually happened. For the most part, though, my characters are fictional. You won't find Ginny Nolan, Virginia Hightower, or Nicholas Bennett on any passenger list for #25, the passenger train.

You would find references to Lucius Anderson, though. He really was the porter on the sleeping car Winnipeg. And Mrs. Bailets did run the hotel at Wellington (along with her husband). Although the manner in which I've portrayed her is all my own, one detail is based on my reference materials: the fact that, even in the dead of winter, the dining room of her hotel was graced with fresh green plants.

About the Author

CAMERON DOKEY lives in Seattle, Washington. One of the things she liked best about writing this book was that she finally got to do a piece about the place that's now her "home state." That's probably the reason she did her best to give this love story a happy ending!

Cameron has one husband and three cats, and is the author of over a dozen young adult novels. Her favorite read is J.R.R. Tolkien's trilogy, *The Lord of the Rings*. Her favorite TV show is *Buffy the Vampire Slayer.*

When she's not writing, Cameron likes to work in the garden and is learning to quilt. She also makes the best chocolate birthday cakes on the entire planet. Cameron is incredibly excited that *Washington Avalanche, 1910* will be published not quite 100 years after the events which inspired the story.

Bullying.
Threats.
Bullets.

Locker searches? Metal detectors?

Fight back without fists.

fight for your rights:
take a stand against violence

. . . A GIRL BORN
WITH THE FEAR GENE

FEARLESS™

A NEW SERIES BY
FRANCINE PASCAL

A TITLE AVAILABLE EVERY MONTH

**From Pocket Pulse
Published by Pocket Books**